WORLD HISTORY

RELIGION AND WORLD CONFLICT

HOLY WARS THROUGHOUT HISTORY

By Caroline Kennon

Portions of this book originally appeared in *Religion and World Conflict* by Don Nardo.

Published in 2019 by
Lucent Press, an Imprint of Greenhaven Publishing, LLC
353 3rd Avenue
Suite 255
New York, NY 10010

Copyright © 2019 Greenhaven Press, a part of Gale, Cengage Learning
Gale and Greenhaven Press are registered trademarks used herein under license.

All new materials copyright © 2019 Lucent Press, an Imprint of Greenhaven Publishing, LLC.

All rights reserved. No part of this book may be reproduced in any form without permission in writing from the publisher, except by a reviewer.

Designer: Deanna Paternostro
Editor: Siyavush Saidian

Cataloging-in-Publication Data

Names: Kennon, Caroline.
Title: Religion and world conflict: holy wars throughout history / Caroline Kennon.
Description: New York : Lucent Press, 2019. | Series: World history | Includes index.
Identifiers: ISBN 9781534563872 (pbk.) | ISBN 9781534563858 (library bound) | ISBN 9781534563865 (ebook)
Subjects: LCSH: Violence–Religious aspects–Juvenile literature. | Religion and international relations–Juvenile literature. | War–Religious aspects–Juvenile literature.
Classification: LCC BL65.V55 K46 2019 | DDC 201'.7273–dc23

CPSIA compliance information: Batch #BS18KL: For further information contact Greenhaven Publishing LLC, New York, New York at 1-844-317-7404.

Please visit our website, www.greenhavenpublishing.com. For a free color catalog of all our high-quality books, call toll free 1-844-317-7404 or fax 1-844-317-7405.

Contents

Foreword

History books are often filled with names and dates—words and numbers for students to memorize for a test and forget once they move on to another class. However, what history books should be filled with are great stories, because the history of our world is filled with great stories. Love, death, violence, heroism, and betrayal are not just themes found in novels and movie scripts. They are often the driving forces behind major historical events.

When told in a compelling way, fact is often far more interesting—and sometimes far more unbelievable—than fiction. World history is filled with more drama than the best television shows, and all of it really happened. As readers discover the incredible truth behind the triumphs and tragedies that have impacted the world since ancient times, they also come to understand that everything is connected. Historical events do not exist in a vacuum. The stories that shaped world history continue to shape the present and will undoubtedly shape the future.

The titles in this series aim to provide readers with a comprehensive understanding of pivotal events in world history. They are written with a focus on providing readers with multiple perspectives to help them develop an appreciation for the complexity of the study of history. There is no set lens through which history must be viewed, and these titles encourage readers to analyze different viewpoints to understand why a historical figure acted the way they did or why a contemporary scholar wrote what they did about a historical event. In this way, readers are able to sharpen their critical-thinking skills and apply those skills in their history classes. Readers are aided in this pursuit by formally documented quotations and annotated bibliographies, which encourage further research and debate.

Many of these quotations come from carefully selected primary sources, including diaries, public records, and contemporary research and writings. These valuable primary sources help readers hear the voices of those who directly experienced historical events, as well as the voices of biographers and historians who provide a unique perspective on familiar topics. Their voices all help history come alive in a vibrant way.

As students read the titles in this series, they are provided with clear context in the form of maps, timelines, and informative text. These elements give them the basic facts they need to fully appreciate the high drama that is history.

The study of history is difficult at times—not because of all the information that needs to be memorized, but because of the challenging questions it asks us. How could something as horrible as the Holocaust happen? Why would religious leaders use torture during the Inquisition? Why does ISIS have so many followers? The information presented in each title gives readers the tools they need to confront these questions and participate in the debates they inspire.

As we pore over the stories of events and eras that changed the world, we come to understand a simple truth: No one can escape being a part of history. We are not bystanders; we are active participants in the stories that are being created now and will be written about in history books decades and even centuries from now. The titles in this series help readers gain a deeper appreciation for history and a stronger understanding of the connection between the stories of the past and the stories they are a part of right now.

SETTING THE SCENE: A TIMELINE

725

Muslims invade Christian France.

732

Frankish leader Charles Martel defeats the invading Muslims at the Battle of Tours and stops the invasion from gaining ground.

1095–1291

European Christians launch the Crusades, a series of battles against Muslims for control of the Holy Land near Palestine.

1347–1351

The Black Death, a devastating plague, kills millions across Europe; thousands of Jewish people are killed after being accused of poisoning water supplies.

1517–1648

The Protestant Reformation begins after Martin Luther declares the Catholic Church corrupt; European Catholics and Protestants engage in the Thirty Years' War for political power.

1649

King Charles I is executed, and Oliver Cromwell takes control of England with his Puritan party.

1692–1693

The Salem witch trials in Massachusetts result in 20 deaths.

1941

A mass extermination of Jewish people begins at Auschwitz, a concentration camp run by Nazis during World War II.

1988–2001

Osama bin Laden organizes the group of Muslim soldiers who later become known as al-Qaeda; Saddam Hussein, president of Iraq, invades Kuwait, which eventually results in his removal from power; nearly 3,000 people are killed in the September 11 terror attacks, orchestrated by the Islamic extremists of al-Qaeda.

2003

Abu Musab al-Zarqawi forms the extremist Muslim group that later becomes known as ISIS, or the Islamic State in Iraq and Syria.

2017

U.S. President Donald Trump introduces increased travel restrictions, making it difficult for Muslims to enter the United States; ISIS continues fighting against Western countries.

INTRODUCTION

EXPLAINING RELIGIOUS WAR

Those who participate in and advocate for organized religion often argue that it guides individuals toward a sense of morality. Morality is essential for the human race to thrive and succeed because knowing the difference between right and wrong means knowing the difference between helping or harming others. Therefore, the fact that religion should be directly associated with doing the right thing makes religious war seem like an impossible contradiction: The violence and destruction of war should be the complete opposite of the moral love of religion. Historically, however, religion has been closely related to many wars and deaths.

For thousands of years, wars have been waged and armies have gone to battle with both sides thinking that they alone were fighting for the good of their religion. Violence is waged in order to spread a particular faith, while aiming to eliminate any existing alternative beliefs. This happened in the holy wars of the Crusades, which began in 1095 with the objective of capturing Muslim places and making them Christian. It continues to this day with the Islamic State bombing traditionally Christian countries in order to demonstrate the power and righteousness of Islamic extremism.

The overwhelmingly large majority of religious people practice compassion and kindness, and they would never kill in the name of their faith. However, it is clear that religion and conflict have a certain partnership throughout history, and it is one not always easily understood: If religion promotes morality, is it not true that all religious people should accept one another with tolerance, if not love, despite any differences?

September 11, 2001

On the morning of September 11, 2001,

The attack on the World Trade Center is a tragic example of religiously motivated warfare.

millions of people gathered in front of television sets across the United States and around the world to witness an unprecedented catastrophe. Most were horrified and stunned by images of two hijacked planes crashing with explosive impact into the World Trade Center towers in New York City. These structures, then among the tallest in the world, burst into flame. Within two hours, as hundreds of courageous firefighters attempted to rescue people trapped on the upper floors, both towers suddenly collapsed into gigantic piles of rubble and thick dust. Meanwhile, a third hijacked plane struck the Pentagon near Washington, D.C., and a fourth crashed in rural Pennsylvania. In all, nearly 3,000 people died in these tragic attacks. This event and subsequent American efforts to find and punish those responsible marked the beginning of a conflict that many in the West call the war on terrorism.

A disturbing revelation emerged in the days following the September 11 disaster: American, British, and other international investigators found that these mass murders had been committed in the name of religion. Nineteen young Muslim men from Saudi Arabia and other Middle Eastern nations had committed the crimes as part of a carefully crafted plan conceived by the leaders of the fundamentalist Islamic terrorist group known as al-Qaeda, which can be translated as "the Base" or "the Foundation." Al-Qaeda had carried out these attacks while invoking the blessings and calling on the name of Allah, the god of Islam. A long letter later found in the belongings of one of the hijackers stated in part:

> *Do not seem confused or show signs of nervous tension. Be happy, optimistic, calm because you are heading for a deed that God loves and will accept ... you are heading toward eternal paradise ... Remember that this is a battle for the sake of God ... When the confrontation begins ... shout Allahu Akbar! ["God is great"] because this strikes fear in the hearts of the non-believers.*[1]

In the Name of the "Father"

In the wake of the September 11 attacks, many Americans and other Westerners were appalled, confused, and disheartened by reports that such a terrible act had been committed in God's name. Most people living in Western countries belong to organized religions, including Christianity, Judaism, Islam, and others. The majority of believers think that taking a human life is a terrible sin and strictly against God's wishes. However, historians and others familiar with the long saga of humanity were quick to point out that killing in the name of religion is nothing new. Some suggested that people in today's progressive, industrialized countries—including the United States and most European nations—had long suffered from a kind of collective historical amnesia. Wars, battles, and assassinations committed in the name of God have occurred repeatedly in all corners of the globe throughout recorded history. As one of these scholars, James A. Haught, argued,

> *Time after time, in widely varied ways, faith spurs some believers to commit barbarism. The problem is a monster with a thousand faces. Millions of people think religion makes believers kind and brotherly, but there's an opposite side, a deeply disturbing one. Why does religion [encourage] some people to kill? No satisfactory answer has ever been found.*[2]

Nobel Prize–winning physicist Steven Weinberg has echoed the same thought, adding that religiously motivated killing can often occur within a given faith as well as between rival faiths:

> *Certainly good causes have sometimes been mobilized under the banner of religion, but ... it's more often been the motivation for us to kill each other—not only for people of one religion to kill those of another, but even within religions. After all, it was a [Muslim] who killed [Egyptian president Anwar] Sadat [in 1981]. It was a devout Jew who killed [Israeli prime minister Yitzhak] Rabin [in 1995]. It was a devout Hindu who killed [Indian nationalist and pacifist spiritual leader Mohandas] Gandhi [in 1948]. And this has been going on for centuries and centuries.*[3]

Although Islamic extremism is often seen as the largest global religious threat in the 21st century, historically, Christians have been guilty of many acts of war against various religions. Among the more infamous of these were the Crusades, a series of medieval wars in which Christians and Muslims slaughtered each other for possession of the sacred city of Jerusalem and the holy lands surrounding it. Christians have also killed countless Jews throughout medieval and modern times and battled other Christians in France, England, and other European countries, including the Protestant and Catholic conflicts in Northern Ireland.

What Goes into a Holy War

While the specific circumstances of these conflicts and massacres vary, nearly all of them have basic traits and characteristics in common. First, each involves some clearly defined religious goal. In the case of the September 11 attacks, for instance, al-Qaeda's main goal was to force the United States and other Western countries to remove their troops and military bases from Islamic countries in the Middle East. Sometimes, the main religious goal is in line with political

Osama bin Laden was the mastermind behind the September 11, 2001, attacks on the United States.

or economic motivations. In the case of al-Qaeda, its leaders used violence to weaken the economies of Western nations and expose their democratic systems as vulnerable.

Second, nearly all holy wars and religiously motivated killings are led and sanctioned by a central, often militant, figure. Al-Qaeda's chief leader was the Muslim fundamentalist Osama bin Laden, the son of a wealthy Saudi businessman. Most of his public statements claimed in one way or another that al-Qaeda's violent acts were the will of Allah. Many followers of al-Qaeda around the world thought bin Laden was chosen by God to convert countries such as the United States and those in Europe to Islam. Similarly, another infamous religious leader, 17th century English politician Oliver Cromwell, believed God chose him to lead. Under the banner of God, Cromwell, a devout Puritan (a conservative Protestant branch), made himself England's absolute ruler and persecuted Catholics.

A third common characteristic of religious wars has been the promise of rewards or salvation for those who take part. The 19 suicide hijackers who piloted the doomed planes on September 11 did so believing that Allah would reward them in the afterlife. During the Crusades, bishops and other church leaders promised Christian soldiers that they would get into heaven by massacring Jewish and Muslim men, women, and children.

Motivating the Faithful

In addition to promising their followers salvation, leaders of religious wars have used various justifications to motivate acts of brutality. Leaders have often told their followers that resorting to violence can help spread the faith, that holy sites are in need of protection from infidels, or that past acts of violence or blasphemy need to be avenged. However, the most common and powerful motivation for religious violence has been the notion that killing is God's will. To prove that this is so, the leaders of holy wars typically fall back on the most aggressive or vengeful passages from sacred writings. Sections of the Koran, Islam's holy book, for instance, have been invoked to justify *jihad*, an Arabic word often translated as "holy war." One passage of the Koran reads,

> *Allah will bring to nothing the deeds of those who disbelieve [in him] … the unbelievers follow falsehood, while the faithful follow truth from their Lord … When you meet the unbelievers in the battlefield strike off their heads and, when you have laid them low, bind your captives firmly … Believers, if you help Allah, Allah will help you and make you strong.*[4]

Islam is not the only faith whose scriptures are cited as justifications for war and murder. Through the centuries, numerous Christian zealots have

Shown here is a version of the Koran from the 19th century.

fallen back on passages from the Bible to defend or rationalize their violent acts. Often cited in this regard are the following verses from the Book of Deuteronomy:

> *When you go near a city to fight against it, then proclaim an offer of peace to it … if the city will not make peace with you … then you shall besiege it. And when the Lord your God delivers it into your hands, you shall strike every male in it with the edge of the sword. But the women, the little ones, the livestock, and all that is in the city, all its spoil, you shall plunder for yourself.*[5]

Obviously, the Koran, the Bible, and other widely esteemed religious writings contain numerous passages that advocate positive paths, such as peace, brotherhood, and forgiveness. However, many people have consistently chosen instead to embrace these harsher divine directives. Inspired by them, individuals have committed violent acts or declared war in the name of their religion. Despite religion often producing good and constructive results, religious fervor has also tragically played a major role in world conflicts.

CHAPTER ONE

RELIGIOUS FUNDAMENTALISM

In 1766, in Abbeville, France, a woman accused a 19-year-old named Jean-François, chevalier de la Barre, of keeping his hat on while a religious procession passed by. This act, considered extremely offensive by some, was all the proof a local Catholic priest needed to then accuse de la Barre of defacing a crucifix on a bridge in the town. Based on this accusation, de la Barre was tortured until he confessed and then sentenced to be executed by both a beheading and burning at the stake. Although Voltaire, the influential French philosopher, protested loudly when he heard about the sentencing, and French authorities offered to reduce de la Barre's sentence, the Catholic Church had too much power. The French authorities were afraid for their own lives if they were to pardon de la Barre, so the young man was executed.

The execution of de la Barre was an example of the violent capabilities of religious fundamentalism. Fundamentalists believe in a very literal interpretation—typically very old and conservative—of scripture. Fundamentalists assume that those who disagree with them and do not accept these conservative beliefs are wrong or evil. The French priests who condemned de la Barre to death considered failing to remove a hat during a religious procession a crime against God. They feared that this act of disrespect would weaken the faith—and probably the obedience—of the whole community, and therefore de la Barre needed to be held accountable. The more the French Christians feared the wrath of God, the more power the religious governments had over the people. Like many fundamentalists, these French priests strongly opposed religious diversity—all citizens were forced to conform to their designated religious views.

Every religion has aspects of fundamentalism, but it is important to distinguish fundamentalists from the

Symbols of God, such as this French crucifix, are treated with great reverence.

SUPERNATURAL CHRISTIANITY

Today, the word "fundamentalism" is often used in a negative context. However, the Baptist pastor who popularized the term in the early 1900s intended it to be a positive word. He wrote a series of essays titled *The Fundamentals*, in which he discussed the importance of the Bible's more supernatural concepts. He wanted Christians to believe in miracles. He thought that interpretations of Christianity were becoming too rationalistic:

> *This rationalism, when full grown, scorns the miracles of the Old Testament, sets aside the virgin birth of our Lord as a thing unbelievable, laughs at the credulity of those who accept many of the New Testament miracles, reduces the resurrection of our Lord to the fact that death did not end his existence, and sweeps away the promises of his second coming as an idle dream.*[1]

1. Quoted in Matt Thompson, "The Origins of 'Fundamentalism,'" *The Atlantic*, June 30, 2015. www.theatlantic.com/entertainment/archive/2015/06/the-origins-of-fundamentalism/397238.

majority of those who practice religion. Even within the fundamentalists, many would never consider committing murder or mutilation. However, some have resorted to violence when they felt that a core aspect of their faith had been threatened. In the 21st century, the most famous example of fundamentalism, or extremism, is the Islamic State in Iraq and Syria, or ISIS. ISIS believes that the whole world must practice Islam and that it must terrorize everyone who holds different views than it does. It is very important to remember that, similarly to those calling for the death of de la Barre, ISIS represents an extremely small percentage of a religious group.

The Beginnings of Islam

Muslim fundamentalism has been around since the seventh and eighth centuries. Islam originated in Arabia in the early 600s when the prophet Muhammad began attracting followers in Medina, a city situated 200 miles (320 kilometers) north of Mecca, which is now considered Islam's holiest city. Muhammad claimed that he had an encounter with the angel Gabriel, who gave him the word of Allah. These messages became the basis for Islam's holiest book, the Koran. Over the next few years, the new faith, based on the teachings of the Koran, spread to Mecca and other parts of the Middle East.

The Islamic religion as it is known today was established by the prophet Muhammad.

THE BOY MUHAMMAD

Muhammad was not always a powerful prophet. He was born around the year 570 into the Quraysh tribe in what is now Saudi Arabia. As a child, he was called al-Amin, which means "the one you can trust." Because his parents died when he was young, the boy was raised first by his grandfather and then his uncle. As a young man, al-Amin became a merchant, married, and had six children. His life was good, but he soon grew dissatisfied. He began to go on long retreats to mountain caves outside of Mecca. Not long after this, according to scripture, he received a series of miraculous visions of the angel Gabriel. This happened to Muhammad several times until he began relaying the messages from the angel to his tribe. These messages are what would become Islam's most sacred teachings in the Koran.

Muhammad, who came to be called the Prophet, died in 632, but Islam survived and grew. The Prophet's most zealous followers decided that the best way to spread the faith was to seize neighboring lands. In 634, the new caliph (or successor to Muhammad), Umar (or Omar) I, whipped his Arab troops into a state of religious and patriotic fervor. Syria fell to these troops in 636, Mesopotamia (now Iraq) fell between 637 and 641, Egypt in 642, and Iran in 651. Arab armies next surged across North Africa and entered Spain, where they established an Islamic state in 711.

During these conquests, the invaders killed many who openly opposed them, but large portions of native populations were spared. Also, contrary to some popular accounts, the Muslim conquerors did not force all the defeated peoples to convert to Islam. Historians have pointed out that the non-Muslim subjects of these lands were second-class citizens, paying a higher rate of taxation, suffering from certain social disabilities, and only on a few rare occasions subjected to open persecution. However, for the most part, "they enjoyed the free exercise of their religion, normal property rights, and were very frequently employed in the service of the state."[6] Nevertheless, these non-Muslim peoples no longer controlled their own destiny. As time went on, most of them ended up converting to the faith of their conquerors: Islam. Some did so because it had become the dominant religion. Others converted so that they would be able to reap the economic benefits enjoyed by Muslims.

These early Muslim fundamentalists found that striking fear into their followers—and potential converts—contributed to the success of the Muslim Arab conquests, as well as to the longevity of the Islamic empire. Unquestioning belief in Allah and rigid observance of the principles laid down in the Koran helped bolster the determination and courage of Arab tribesmen who were often ill-equipped and outnumbered by their enemies. It also established the Koran's authority as the source of all truth and wisdom, which minimized the influence of (and possible competition from) rival sects. Elements of this narrow fundamentalist outlook remain alive and well among some groups of followers today, especially those who try to achieve their goals by advocating and committing violence.

Islam in Europe

The militant Muslims of the early eighth century believed that it was their duty to bring all known lands into the Islamic empire. To this end, after overrunning Spain, the Arab armies regrouped and began to move northward into what is now France. The long-term goal was to bring all of Europe under Arab rule and, hopefully, to convert the Europeans to Islam. If this goal had been achieved, much of the history of the world would have been radically different.

At first, the Arab invaders, commanded by the governor of Muslim Spain, Abdul Rahman al-Ghafiqi, enjoyed some successes. Al-Ghafiqi and his troops infiltrated France and raided the town of Autun, about 200 miles (320 km) southeast of Paris, in 725. In the following year, Carcassonne (in southern France) and Nîmes (in southeastern France, near the Mediterranean coast) fell to the Arabs. At the time, the Franks, former Germanic tribesmen who had settled in France during the preceding two centuries, were divided into rival groups with separate leaders. This lack of unity weakened the Franks' military and gave the invaders an important advantage. It appeared that the Arabs might overrun the region and then move on into Germany and other neighboring lands.

Then, around 732, one of the Frankish leaders, Charles Martel, gathered as many Frankish soldiers as possible in the hopes of halting the Arab advance. Martel also managed to convince troops from another strong Germanic tribe, the Burgundians, to join his cause. By this time, al-Ghafiqi had reached Poitiers (west of central France) and was moving north toward Tours. Hearing that the Franks were speeding toward him, he led his troops eastward. Somewhere to the east of Poitiers and Tours (the exact location remains unknown), the two armies met in what turned out to be one of the most decisive battles in history.

How exactly the Battle of Tours was fought is uncertain. Some evidence suggests that Martel arranged his foot soldiers, or infantry, in a huge square

This painting by Charles de Steuben shows Charles Martel defeating al-Ghafiqi in the Battle of Tours.

and that the Arabs were unable to break through the formation. A surviving Arab text describes the fate of the Muslim leader:

> *Near the river Loire the two great [armies] of the two languages and the two creeds [Christianity and Islam] were set in array against each other … The Moslem [Muslim] horsemen dashed fierce and frequent forward against the battalions of the Franks, who resisted manfully, and many fell dead on either side until the going down of the sun … many of the Moslems were fearful for the safety of the [treasures] which they had stored in their tents [and] several squadrons of the Moslem horsemen rode off to protect their tents … And while [al-Ghafiqi] strove to [stop them], and to lead them back to battle, the warriors of the Franks came around him, and he was pierced through with many spears, so that he died. Then all the [army] fled before the enemy.*[7]

With their leader dead and the battle lost, the Arabs retreated south toward their Spanish kingdom. Martel and his men had saved their own country, and likely most of the rest of Europe, from Muslim domination. However, the

Arabs continued their raids into southern France for some time to come and remained a potential threat to Europe for many more centuries. Not until 1492 did the Spanish Christian monarchs Ferdinand and Isabella achieve the surrender of Granada, the last Muslim stronghold in Spain.

Burning the Witches

During the 1400s, with the Arab threat fast receding, Europeans began to encounter another onslaught of violence motivated by fundamentalist beliefs. Priests and other officials of the Catholic Church, led by their leader, the pope in Rome, conducted a series of witch hunts that lasted for about three centuries. During this period, Catholic believers convinced themselves that killing several thousand "witches" was justified in the eyes of God.

Europe's great series of witch hunts originally grew out of the formation and expansion of the Catholic Inquisition. This organization within the church was created in the early 1200s with the goal of stamping out heresy. Heresy was any opposition or lack of adherence to the established religious order and its most basic beliefs. The popes sent out inquisitors, who were a type of detective, to root out, bring to trial, condemn, and—if necessary—execute the supposed enemies of the Catholic faith. The inquisitors came from many different ranks of the priesthood, but a large proportion of them were Dominican monks.

Among the heretics the inquisitors were looking for were "witches." In medieval times, witches were commonly identified as women who were followers of Satan and his dark forces. Among the accusations against witches were that they engaged in inappropriate acts with Satan or his demons, transformed themselves into animals, flew through the sky, made themselves invisible, or tried to corrupt ordinary God-fearing folk. Although a few accused witches were executed in the 1200s and 1300s, the witch hunts became large-scale only after Pope Innocent VIII issued an edict in 1484. This document declared not only that witches were real but that anyone who did not believe in witches was also a heretic. In 1486, two Dominican inquisitors published the *Malleus Maleficarum*, or *The Witches' Hammer*. This infamous guidebook listed the supernatural acts supposedly performed by witches and stated that witches caused disease, destroyed crops, and kidnapped and ate children.

Sanctioned by the popes and their bishops, the Inquisition conducted witch hunts in Germany, France, Italy, Spain, Sweden, Switzerland, and elsewhere in Europe. Other Christian groups also conducted persecutions. These persecutions eventually reached England and the New World—North America. The most famous in the New World took place in 1692 in Salem, part of the Massachusetts Bay Colony.

Most of the accused witches were women whose names had been shouted

The Inquisition's seal included both a cross and a sword.

Many women who were accused of witchcraft were tortured, as shown here.

out by other women being tortured by inquisitors. After their arrest, suspected witches were often subjected to gruesome tortures to force confessions of witchcraft and to reveal the names of new suspects. "The victims were stripped naked [and] shaved of all body hair," one scholar wrote. "Fingernails were pulled out. Red-hot tongs were applied ... Bodies were stretched on racks and wheels ... Virtually every mangled and broken victim confessed—and was executed on the basis of the confession."[8] The practices of forcing confessions and making false accusations made it seem like there was proof that witchcraft existed. It kept Christians in a state of fear that was easily manipulated by the leaders of both church and state.

The hysteria over witchcraft gradually subsided, and by 1700, the number of witches accused and arrested in Europe had decreased dramatically. A few women were still victimized after that, even as the rise of modern science raised major doubts about the authenticity of witchcraft. The last legalized execution of a witch occurred in 1782 in Switzerland. However, the centuries of persecution based on fundamentalist intolerance and paranoia still remain a shameful chapter in the history of the Christian faith.

The Puritans of England

Not long after witch hunts began to spread across Europe, the Protestant Reformation began. In 1517, priest and professor of theology Martin Luther declared that the Roman Catholic Church was likely corrupt. Luther had a problem with the selling of indulgences, which were documents the Catholic Church sold to its followers in exchange for promises that the individuals would get to heaven faster once they died. Luther taught that scripture was the ultimate source of authority and only faith in Jesus could wipe away sin—not the church itself. This laid the groundwork for an anti-Catholic sentiment, which only grew stronger when England's King Henry VIII separated his entire country from the authority of the pope in 1534. Angered by the pope's refusal to grant him a divorce, Henry established the Church of England, a Protestant denomination of Christianity also known as the Anglican Church, and declared himself its supreme leader. Under the new religious order, Catholics, especially wealthy and powerful ones, became increasingly unpopular.

Even as anti-Catholic sentiment grew in England, some devoutly religious Englishmen came to see both the new Church of England and the pope as corrupt and tyrannical. These Protestant fundamentalist minorities wanted to purify the church and reassert the power of the Bible over worldly authority. The order they formed became known as the Puritans. Not surprisingly, both Anglican and Roman Catholic leaders, including the reigning monarchs, resented the Puritans' existence, which resulted in a series of persecutions in the early 1600s. Fleeing these persecutions, some Puritans moved to the Netherlands, while others crossed the Atlantic Ocean and established a North American colony at Plymouth, in what is now the commonwealth of Massachusetts (where some of them were later burned as witches).

Despite the two churches' best efforts, the Puritans persevered and eventually, if briefly, triumphed. Over the years, they gained many sympathizers in Parliament, England's primary government body. Then, in the early 1640s, King Charles I had a major disagreement with Parliament after he attempted to arrest its leaders, including several Puritans. The king's enemies proceeded to form a rival government and raise troops. A bloody four-year-long civil war ensued, during which Oliver Cromwell, a Puritan who had earlier served in Parliament, took charge of the forces opposing the king.

Cromwell and his Puritan followers turned their religious believers into a military organization. The soldiers, who became known as "Ironsides," carried Bibles with them everywhere and sang hymns while marching. All battles were

Martin Luther helped lay the groundwork for anti-Catholic feelings.

Oliver Cromwell led the Puritans against the British and Irish Catholics.

CROMWELL IN IRELAND

Oliver Cromwell recorded his own account of the storming of the Irish city of Drogheda in 1649. After he and his Puritan troops took the city, they massacred thousands of survivors:

> *Although our men that stormed the breaches were forced to recoil [pull back] … being encouraged to recover their loss, they made a second attempt, wherein God was pleased to animate them [and] they got ground of the enemy, and, by the goodness of God, forced him to quit his entrenchments. And, after a very hot dispute, the enemy … gave ground, and our men became masters of [most of the town] … Being in the heat of action, I forbade [my soldiers] to spare any [that] were in arms in the town, and I think that night they put to the sword about two thousand men.*[1]

1. Quoted in J. B. Williams, "Fresh Light on Cromwell at Drogheda," in *The Nineteenth Century and After*, vol. LXXII, July–December 1912. New York, NY: Leonard Scott, p. 480.

preceded by prayers, and any victories were attributed to God, whom the Puritans claimed was on their side. As Cromwell himself stated,

> *A great thing should be done, not by power or might, but by the Spirit of God. And is it not so clearly? That which caused your men to storm [into battle] so courageously … it was the Spirit of God, who gave your men courage and … therewith this happy success. And therefore it is good that God alone have all the glory.*[9]

King Charles lost the civil war, and Parliament set limits on the power of the monarch. Charles, however, was reluctant to stay within these limits, and Cromwell eventually led the radical movement to accuse Charles of treason and sentence him to death. Charles was executed in 1649, by which time Cromwell, with the army under his complete control, had become a dictator.

Puritan Problems

In the years that followed Charles's execution, the remaining Catholics in England and Ireland suffered under the rule of the Puritans, who hated the pope and viewed Catholics as vermin. Led by Cromwell, who now bore the title of Lord Protector, the Puritans crossed into Ireland and began slaughtering Catholics and Protestants who sympathized with the Catholics. After much hard fighting, the city of Drogheda surrendered. Cromwell's troops then sacked the city and massacred thousands of prisoners, including women and priests. Cromwell believed that the violence he committed was done in the name of God and done with divine blessings.

In addition to committing mass murder, the Puritans attempted to remake English society, banning all forms of public entertainment, including dancing and going to the theater. They called such activities wasteful and against God's will. Because of these changes, large numbers of English, including both Catholics and Protestants, came to hate the Puritan regime. After Cromwell died in 1658, there was an enormous backlash. In what came to be called the Restoration, the monarchy was restored and Puritans were driven out of public posts. The Restoration was another in a long line of examples of more moderate—and tolerant—beliefs eventually winning over the forces of fundamentalist extremism.

CHAPTER TWO

RELIGIOUS TERROR

The destruction of the World Trade Center towers in New York City in 2001 is often seen as the symbolic beginning of the modern war on terror. The 19 Muslim men who hijacked airplanes and used them as weapons of mass destruction instantly became faces of terrorism. Terrorism is defined as the use of kidnappings, bombings, assassinations, mass murders, and other violent acts designed to strike fear in a general population, either to bring about or to discourage some kind of political or social change.

Terrorists always have an agenda. In 1972, members of a radical group called Black September infiltrated the Olympic Village in Munich, Germany, took several Israeli athletes hostage, and murdered their captives. The terrorists' demand, one they never achieved, was the release of 200 Palestinians then held in Israeli and German jails. Other terrorist acts have been perpetrated to maintain a social or political status quo. This was the case with the Ku Klux Klan (KKK) in the United States in the late 1800s and 1900s. During this period, KKK members committed thousands of beatings, house burnings, lynchings, and other crimes against African Americans. The KKK's primary goal was to maintain fear among blacks and maintain a racist society in which blacks were treated as inferiors. The KKK is still promoting racist beliefs and practices in the United States today.

What made the September 11 attacks different from the crimes committed by Black September and the KKK was that the hijackers were all Muslims who were largely motivated by religious extremism. The main goal of al-Qaeda, the extremist group to which the pilots of September 11 belonged, is to drive Western "infidels" (meaning those who do not practice Islam) out of Muslim countries and establish Islamic theocracies around the world. In

The Ku Klux Klan violently believes that black Americans are inferior to whites.

perpetrating terror attacks in the United States in 2001, as well as in Spain and other countries soon afterward, the attackers believed they were acting in God's name and with his approval. They expected to be rewarded by Allah in paradise.

Although al-Qaeda awakened the modern world to the threat of religiously motivated terrorism, its goals and methods were far from new. People have been committing terrorist acts in the name of one divine being or another for thousands of years.

The Assassins

One of the most infamous terrorist organizations in history was a group known as the Assassins. The goup's chief goal was to kill well-known and powerful military, religious, or national leaders whom it opposed. The group's name survives in the common term "assassin," used to describe someone who kills a political or powerful figure. The Assassins were a fundamentalist offshoot of the Ismailis, one of several Shiite Muslim groups that formed in the centuries immediately following the death of the prophet Muhammad and the spread of Islam throughout the Middle East. Over time, a small group of Ismailis came to view the caliphs and sultans—the Islamic rulers of the large Middle Eastern cities and kingdoms of the day—as too corrupt. The dissenters held that most of these rulers had abandoned certain basic Islamic principles and therefore must be removed from power. However, the Ismailis who felt this way were relatively few in number. Unable to muster large armies to achieve their aims, they chose instead to form a secretive and deadly organization to terrorize and kill the caliphs and sultans. That organization, eventually named the Assassins, began operations in what are now Syria, Iraq, and Iran in the late 11th century.

The Assassins established several fortresses in remote sites high in mountain ranges, where the armies of the caliphs could not easily find them. The most important and famous of these hideouts was the Eagle's Nest, located in the Iranian highlands. The leader of the organization was called the grand-master, or the Old Man of the Mountain. Next in command were the grand-priors, leaders of individual cells of Assassins in various districts of the Middle East. Most of the Assassins fell into a third group: the Propagandists, consisting of soldiers, laborers, servants, and others who carried out the leaders' orders. Those orders, along with the methods the Assassins employed, followed fairly strict guidelines, which were also set forth by the group's leaders. As one historian explained,

> *The chosen victims were almost invariably the rulers and leaders of the existing order—monarchs, generals, ministers, major religious [figures]. [The Assassins] attacked only the great and powerful, and never harmed ordinary people … Their weapon was almost always the same—the dagger, wielded by the appointed Assassin in person. It is significant that they made virtually no use of such safer weapons as were available to them at the time—the bow and crossbow, missiles [spears and rocks], and poison … The Assassin himself, having struck down his assigned victim, made no attempt to escape, nor was any attempt made to rescue him. On the contrary, to have survived a mission was seen as a disgrace.*[10]

The Assassins are a historic example of terrorism used to achieve a religious objective.

Assassinating for a Change

In 1092, the Assassins succeeded in killing the sultan of Baghdad (now in Iraq), Nizam al-Mulk. They also managed to slay other Middle Eastern Muslim leaders in the years that followed, creating widespread terror among the region's ruling classes. The Assassins also occasionally attacked and killed Christian leaders who were trying to remove Muslims from the Holy Land during the Crusades. In 1192, for example, one of the Assassins killed the European nobleman Conrad of Montferrat, who ruled Christian-held Jerusalem at the time. Additionally, the Assassins were not above making alliances with key foes to further their own objectives. Sometimes, Muslim leaders helped the Assassins kill other Muslim leaders in hopes of getting rid of political or religious rivals. Similarly, Christian crusaders, at times, made alliances with the Assassins because they had mutual enemies—namely, most Muslim leaders. For a while, one powerful group of crusaders, the Knights Templar, had some kind of arrangement with the Syrian Assassins and collected gold and other valuables from them on a regular basis. The purpose of these payments is still uncertain, but it may have been to ensure that Christian armies would leave the Assassins' strongholds alone. This allowed the Assassins to concentrate most of their time and energy on stalking and killing Muslim leaders.

For nearly two centuries, the Assassins were a potent force in Islamic society and often seemed almost invincible. They finally met their match when the Mongols, a nomadic people from central Asia, swept through and conquered the Middle East in the 13th century. In 1257, the Mongols, whose warriors were expert horsemen and fierce fighters, captured and destroyed the Eagle's Nest after reducing many other Assassin fortresses to rubble. The surviving Assassins begged the Templars and some other leading crusaders to take them in. The Assassins even went so far as to offer to convert to Christianity, but the Christian knights refused to help them, and not long afterward, a local sultan eradicated the last of the Assassin mountain fortresses in Syria. Even after their demise, however, the Assassins left behind a formidable, frightening, and influential legacy. "Their movement," one scholar wrote, "was regarded as a profound threat to the existing order … They did not [ultimately] overthrow that existing order … yet the undercurrent of … hope and revolutionary violence which had [encouraged] them flowed on, and their ideals and methods found many imitators [in later ages]."[11]

Thugs

Another medieval group that killed and terrorized society in the name of a deity utilized strangulation, rather

Mongol warriors were often depicted as savage fighters.

A MEDIEVAL CHRISTIAN VIEW OF THE ASSASSINS

After the Christian ruler of Jerusalem, Conrad of Montferrat, was slain by an Assassin in 1192, the crusaders became aware of and fascinated by the Assassins' cult. Several Christian writers of that era commented on the Assassins, sometimes conveying accurate information, but just as often passing on rumors and hearsay. One of these writers, Arnold of Lubeck, stated,

> *This Old Man [of the Mountain] has by his witchcraft so bemused the men of his country, that they neither worship nor believe in any God but himself. Likewise, he entices them in a strange manner, with such hopes and with promises of such pleasures with eternal enjoyment, that they prefer rather to die than to live. Many of them, when standing on a high wall, will jump off at his nod or command, and, shattering their skulls, die a miserable death. The most blessed, so he affirms, are those who shed the blood of men and in revenge for such deeds themselves suffer death.*[1]

1. Quoted in Bernard Lewis, *The Assassins: A Radical Sect in Islam*. New York, NY: Basic Books, 1967, p. 4.

than stabbing, as its signature method of murder. Unlike the Assassins, however, this cult survived and continued to commit crimes well into modern times. These stranglers lived in India and came to be called the Thuggees (from the Hindi word *thag*, meaning "thief," and derived from a Sanskrit word, *sthaga*, meaning "scoundrel" or "concealed"). It became common to call the Thuggees "thugs" for short. When the British gained control of India in the 1800s, the word "thug," meaning a violent criminal, entered the English language. The Thuggees were founded in the 1200s, right about the time that the Assassins were being eradicated by the Mongols. Most Thuggees were Hindus, although a few renegade Muslims and Sikhs supposedly joined the group from time to time.

The standard practice of the Thuggees was for several members—at least 10 and sometimes 100 or more—to lie in wait for travelers on the main roads. They would then pretend to be fellow travelers and gain their

KALI THE DESTROYER

Kali, the Hindu goddess whom the Thuggees believed they were serving, is typically portrayed in Indian art as a violent, forceful deity wielding swords in some of her many hands. Additionally, she is sometimes depicted with a belt or skirt made of human arms and a necklace made of severed human heads. According to some texts, she is married to another important Hindu god—Shiva—who is also a symbol of destruction and death. The name "Kali," itself, can be translated as "She Who Is Black" or "She Who Is Death." The violent and aggressive imagery that is often associated with Kali made the goddess a natural divine mentor of the Thuggee cult.

victims' confidence by conversing with them and even helping them set up camp and cook meals. Then, one of the Thuggees would give a signal to strike. According to some accounts, the code phrase was "bring the tobacco," although there may well have been other signals. Suddenly, quickly, and with frightening efficiency, the attackers would produce yellow scarves, slip them around their victims' necks, and strangle them to death. Afterward, it was also standard practice to make away with the victims' valuables.

The Thuggees were not ordinary thieves and muggers. They strangled people not simply to rob them but also as part of what they viewed as a sacred ritual. Originally, they worshipped and killed in the name of Kali, the Hindu goddess of creation, preservation, and destruction, but very little is known about the secret beliefs of the cult and how its members justified their actions in the goddess's name. What seems fairly certain is that they did not believe they were committing murder when they killed their victims. Rather, they were offering up their victims to Kali as a kind of sacrifice. According to the Thuggees, Kali desired to maintain a mysterious balance of life on Earth, and she promised that both the stranglers and the victims would receive some kind of reward in the afterlife for their offering. Another common belief was that each death carried out by the Thuggees postponed Kali's destruction of the world by a thousand years. This is a major difference between Thuggees and Assassins, for the Thuggees were not trying to achieve any societal or religious change but instead killed for their own personal spiritual gain.

Kali is the Hindu goddess of creation and destruction that Thuggees worshipped.

The terror that these murders sparked in the general population was only a side effect.

The number of people the Thuggees killed over the centuries is uncertain and regularly debated by scholars. Some place the death toll as high as 2 million; others think this estimate is exaggerated and suggest the true toll is likely 1 million or far fewer. Certainly, at the very least, the Thuggees long spread a wave of terror through large portions of India. The terror and carnage might well have continued indefinitely if the British had not intervened in the 1800s. British military units commanded by Captain William Sleeman rooted out, killed, and arrested many Thuggees. Instrumental in the group's downfall was captured Thuggees' common practice of exposing their compatriots. Ironically, this stemmed from the cult's own beliefs. The Thuggees believed that any one of their number who was captured by the authorities was automatically abandoned by Kali. Feeling that he was on his own and would receive no aid from his former comrades, the prisoner usually cooperated with his captors in exchange for lenient treatment. Thus, by about 1890, the long-lived cult of the Thuggees had been largely exterminated.

Historic Terrrorism

Unfortunately, violent acts perpetrated in the name of religious faith did not die out with the Thuggees. The 20th century and early years of the 21st century have seen countless terrorist acts committed by individuals and groups claiming that God inspired or guided them. The infamy of the September 11 attacks and attacks committed by ISIS in the 2010s have given some people the impression that most modern terrorists have been Muslims, but this is inaccurate. In truth, modern terrorists have belonged to nearly every organized religion, including all branches and sects of Christianity, Islam, Hinduism, Sikhism, Shintoism, and even Judaism.

Religious fervor most likely inspired a group of Sikh militants to cause one of the most lethal mass murders ever to occur on an airliner. It was also Canada's worst case of mass murder. On June 22, 1985, a bomb planted on Air India flight 182 from Montreal to London exploded over the Atlantic Ocean. The death toll was 329. Police investigators followed a trail of clues that eventually led to several Sikhs who wanted to draw attention to their extreme religious goals. They were part of a group of Sikhs who sought to create an independent Sikh homeland inside India.

In the early 1990s, a Jewish Israeli named Baruch Goldstein became convinced that the only way to settle the ongoing conflict among Palestinians and Israelis was to terrorize and kill Palestinians. Goldstein believed that God sanctioned any means, even violence, to rid Israel of its enemies. On

Baruch Goldstein was responsible for killing 29 Palestinians, but some saw him as a soldier of God. His tombstone says that he gave his life for the nation of Israel.

February 25, 1994, during Islam's holy month of Ramadan, Goldstein entered the Ibrahim Mosque in the town of Hebron and began firing a gun into a crowd of praying Palestinians. Nearly 30 people were killed, and 150 were wounded before some of the worshippers disarmed Goldstein. Most Israelis

were shocked and condemned the massacre, but a few of the more radical members of Israeli society saw Goldstein as a soldier of God and a martyr. A martyr is someone who dies while fighting for a noble cause. These same extremists spoke out against the Israeli government, saying that its efforts to make peace with the Palestinians were a betrayal of Israel and Jewish people everywhere.

Al-Qaeda Is Born

Although religiously motivated terrorism existed long before Osama bin Laden and the Islamic State, this particular brand of terror is often what affects the modern world. The crimes committed by al-Qaeda's operatives began making news in the 1990s. The series of attacks orchestrated by al-Qaeda in Africa, Spain, the United States, Britain, Indonesia, and elsewhere made it one of the most feared terrorist groups in modern history. Al-Qaeda was established by Osama bin Laden, a Saudi who had gone to Afghanistan to fight the Soviets after they invaded in 1979. To understand the roots and goals of al-Qaeda, one must go back to the violence in Soviet-occupied Afghanistan.

During the Cold War between the United States and Soviet Union, the United States and Pakistan wanted to help the Afghans drive the Soviets out of their home country. Backed by American and Pakistani funding, a group of Arabs and other Muslims formed an anti-Soviet resistance movement whose fighters were called the mujahideen. Bin Ladin, who hailed from an extremely wealthy and famous Saudi family, became one of the leading mujahideen fighters. In

1988, he formed and led a subgroup of these fighters that later became known as al-Qaeda. Eventually, Afghanistan proved to be a hazardous situation for the Soviets, who suffered heavy causalities and withdrew from the country in 1989. At that time, many of the mujahideen, including bin Laden, decided that they wanted to fight for other causes in which they felt Muslims were being wronged or oppressed. It did not take long for such a situation, in their eyes, to materialize. In 1991, the United States invaded Iraq with the purpose of forcing Iraqi dictator Saddam Hussein to withdraw from Kuwait. Bin Laden and his followers detested Saddam and supported driving him out. However, they were bitterly opposed to the presence of U.S. troops using Saudi territory to launch their attacks on Saddam. Because the Americans were considered infidels, bin Laden said, their presence violated soil sacred to all Muslims. When bin Laden publicly opposed his government's policy, the Saudi government revoked his citizenship and expelled him.

After his banishment, bin Laden and al-Qaeda gained an increasing hatred for the United States and other Western countries, convinced that these nations wanted to dominate and subjugate Muslim countries. In both writing and in the media, al-Qaeda spokesmen condemned the West, often accusing Americans and European countries of crimes they never committed. This statement from the organization's training manual reflects the beliefs of its members:

> *Those apostate [non-Muslim] rulers threw thousands of [Muslim] youth in gloomy jails and detention centers that were equipped with the most modern torture devices and [manned with] experts in oppression and torture … The [Western] rulers did not stop there; they started to fragment the essence of the Islamic [global community] by trying to eradicate its Moslem identity. Thus, they started spreading godless and atheistic views among the youth.*[12]

Al-Qaeda versus the West

At first, al-Qaeda based itself in Sudan, whose sympathetic government allowed the organization to thrive. In 1996, however, responding to mounting pressure from the United States and other Western countries, Sudan ordered bin Laden and his followers to leave. They quickly made a new base for themselves in Afghanistan, then under a strict Islamic regime controlled by Muslim fundamentalists called the Taliban. In bases located in remote areas of Afghanistan, al-Qaeda trained Muslims from around the world in the tactics and ideology of terror.

The purpose of this new army of terrorists soon became clear. In February 1998, bin Laden and his associate,

CONDEMNING THE WEST

Filled with distorted or unsubstantiated information and misleading statements, the al-Qaeda training manual gives a clear idea of how the organization's leaders fill the minds of recruits with the "evils" of Western, non-Muslim societies:

> *Martyrs were killed, women were widowed, children were orphaned, men were handcuffed, chaste women's heads were shaved, harlots' heads were crowned, atrocities were inflicted on the innocent, gifts were given to the wicked … After the fall of our orthodox caliphates on March 3, 1924 … our Islamic nation was afflicted with apostate rulers who took over in the Moslem nation … Muslims have endured all kinds of harm, oppression, and torture at their hands … They [the rulers] tried, using every means and [kind of] seduction, to produce a generation of young men that did not know [anything] except what they [the rulers] want, did not say except what they [the rulers] think about, did not live except according to their [the rulers'] way … However, majestic Allah turned their deception back on them, as a large group of those young men who were raised by them [the rulers] woke up from their sleep and returned to Allah, regretting and repenting. [They] realized that Islam is not just performing rituals but a complete system: Religion and government, worship and Jihad [holy war], ethics and dealing with people, and the Koran and sword.*[1]

1. Quoted in Dale L. June, "A Manifesto of War and Hate: A Look Inside an al-Qaeda Manual" in *Terrorism and Homeland Security: Perspectives, Thoughts, and Opinions*, Dale L. June, ed. Boca Raton, FL: CRC Press, 2010, p. 53.

Ayman al-Zawahiri, issued a fatwa, an Islamic legal decree sanctioned and delivered by religious authorities. It stated in part:

> *To kill the Americans and their allies—civilians and military—is an individual duty for every Muslim who can do it in any country in which it is possible to do it … in order for their armies to move out of all the lands of Islam, defeated and unable to threaten any Muslim. This is in accordance with the words of Almighty Allah … We—with Allah's help—call on every Muslim who believes in Allah and wishes to be rewarded to comply with Allah's order to kill the Americans.*[13]

Not long after this statement was released, al-Qaeda's terrorist attacks began. In August 1998, its operatives set off bombs in the U.S. embassies

Some Islamic extremists have been trained to commit violence against non-Muslims.

in the African countries of Tanzania and Kenya. Several hundred people were killed, and more than 4,000 were injured in the blasts. Al-Qaeda operatives also bombed an American ship, the USS *Cole*, which was then anchored in a harbor in Yemen. Seventeen American sailors died, and another 39 were wounded in this attack.

These terrorist attacks put al-Qaeda on the map, making it clear that the organization was both ruthless and dangerous—to be taken seriously. However, almost no one was prepared for the horrors on September 11, 2001. The operation had been carefully planned for years: Several of the hijackers had entered and lived in the United States for years, and some had taken flying lessons so that they could pilot the planes after they hijacked them. Four commercial passenger airliners were hijacked on September 11. One crashed into the World Trade Center's North Tower at 8:46 a.m.;

the second struck the South Tower at 9:03 a.m.; the third plane flew into the Pentagon, near Washington, D.C., at 9:37 a.m.; and the fourth crashed in a southwestern Pennsylvania field at 10:03 a.m., apparently after its passengers tried to subdue the hijackers. After September 11, bin Laden lied and claimed that he and al-Qaeda had had nothing to do with the carnage, but he later admitted his involvement on Arab television. It became clear that to take responsibility for the terror would only increase its effectiveness.

The Islamic State

The modern face of terrorism has changed since Osama bin Laden and Afghanistan. The influence that al-Qaeda had on Muslims reached far across the Middle East. In 1999, a Jordanian Sunni man named Abu Musab al-Zarqawi traveled to Afghanistan to seek al-Qaeda's money and recruits to fund a revolution in the Fertile Crescent, the land from the eastern Mediterranean to Iraq. Al-Zarqawi was a career criminal. He practiced Salafism, including a hatred of Western cultures and the Shiites (also called Shia), the second-largest branch of Islam next to the Sunnis. Although their opinions differed in some ways, bin Laden saw al-Zarqawi as a potentially useful ally and gave him the money to develop a jihad training camp in Herat, Afghanistan. After September 11, the United States bombed the city of Kandahar, Afghanistan, killing bin Laden's military planner and ending the Taliban's rule. After this, al-Zarqawi found himself fleeing to Iraq.

By 2003, al-Zarqawi had established a group called Monotheism and Jihad,

ISIS's flag is an international symbol of hatred and violence.

which had killed 111 people in bombings of the Jordan embassy and United Nations headquarters in Baghdad, Iraq. This group then became known as al-Qaeda in Iraq (AQI). Al-Zarqawi was also receiving the support of Saddam Hussein's anti-Shiite government. Most of Islam teaches that it is a sin for Muslims to hate other Muslims, but al-Zarqawi preached that any Muslim who shaved his beard, wore Western clothing, or voted in any election—even for a Muslim leader—should be put to death. He believed all 200 million Shiites deserved to die. He posted a video online showing his face to the world, claiming that he would create an Islamic state, and it would be the beginning of the end of the world. Al-Zarqawi was killed in June 2006 when the U.S. Air Force dropped a pair of massive bombs on his hideout 20 miles (32 km) north of Baghdad.

Fundamentalist Islam would prove it could not be destroyed by bombs alone, however. Four months after al-Zarqawi's death, the remaining members of AQI told Iraqi Muslims that they had a new leader, named Abu Omar al-Baghdadi, and that they would now be officially known as the Islamic State of Iraq. This new leader, however, and his right hand man, Abu Ayyub al-Masri, were not good leaders. They did not communicate or manage very well. It seemed like Iraq might finally get some relief: In early 2007, 2,500 civilians were killed each month, but by the end of 2008, that number dropped down to 500. An American/Iraqi raid in April 2010 succeeded in killing both al-Masri and al-Baghdadi. Despite this success, another group of leaders emerged almost immediately.

In May 2010, the head of the Islamic State as of 2017, Abu Bakr al-Baghdadi, took command of the faithful. This newest al-Baghdadi was a scholar of the Koran who had spent a good deal of time in prison for being associated with fundamentalist organizations. Being put in prison had the opposite effect on extremists than the United States was aiming for; the prisons were known as "Jihadi universities" because they grouped together large numbers of potential extremists, making it possible for them to learn and network with each other. Under al-Baghdadi, the Islamic State flourished. It grew and attracted thousands more Muslims to its cause—which is to "purify" the world by killing almost everyone.

Tens of thousands of Muslims have immigrated to areas in Iraq and Syria occupied by ISIS. The Internet helps recruit them, and they come into the organization ready to fight and intending to die for the cause. Thousands of Iraqis and Syrians have died, both as victims and as suicidal terrorists. A United Nations report in 2016 estimated that ISIS holds 3,500 people as slaves. The terror that haunts the rest of the world is random but very effective. Individual members of ISIS carry out acts of destructive violence and murder in order to both send a message and work toward the goal of destroying the world of non-Muslims. In November 2015, 130 people were killed by attacks in Paris. In March 2016, 32 people were killed in Brussels,

Belgium. Other attacks directed or inspired by ISIS have occurred around the world, including in the United States. These attacks generate feelings of terror and anger—which is exactly what the Islamic State wants. ISIS wants the Western world to hate Muslims because this will prove to potential members that the Western world is the enemy of Islam, which will increase its recruitment so it can repeat this destructive cycle.

CHAPTER THREE

ONE NATION, UNDER GOD

Religious devotion has been linked with political power throughout history: The wars that the ancient Assyrian kings waged to gain control of the land that is now Iraq in the first millennium BC were fought in the name of their god, Ashur. In Italy in 312, Constantine, a Roman soldier, called on God to help him dethrone the current emperor. The Crusades saw Christians and Muslims both claiming divine rights to the same land for nearly 200 years. The fighting between Christians and Protestants during the Thirty Years' War left at least 3 million people dead, all to determine which denomination of Christianity would hold the most power.

Modern history continues to see religiously motivated struggles for power. Israel has been at the center of a violent fight between Muslims and Jews for rights to land. Christians and Muslims fought in Sudan in the 1950s for political power. Most recently, ISIS has insisted that Allah is on its side when it comes to geographic control. In 2014, the Muslim terrorist organization controlled more than 34,000 square miles (88,000 sq km) in the countries of Syria and Iraq. This is a little smaller than the size of the state of Maine. Muslims believe that a true heir to Muhammad is its caliph and the area that he rules is called a caliphate. In order for the caliphate to be legitimate, it must not only hold land but also continue to actively grow the size of its territory. ISIS took this territory by force, and many have died or lived under extreme cruelty. This further demonstrates the connection between religious extremism and political power.

Christian Crusaders

The hatred and rivalry between Christians and Muslims in modern Sudan echoes the many violent episodes that occurred during the medieval Crusades. The current violence in Sudan has been instigated mainly by Muslims against Christians, while the holy wars of the Crusades, in contrast, were primarily instigated by Christians against Muslims. These conflicts started in 1095 by Pope Urban II, leader of the Western Christian Church centered in Rome. Urban knew that the holy city of Jerusalem had long been under Arabic Muslim rule. The Muslims had captured the city in 638 during their great jihad. The pope also knew that the Arab Muslims, who revered Jesus Christ as one of their prophets, had long allowed Christian pilgrims to visit Jerusalem without trouble. In 1071, however, a different Muslim group, the Seljuk Turks, had captured Jerusalem and began taxing and sometimes mistreating Christian pilgrims. Urban felt that he had to do something to aid these pilgrims.

It was the way the pope tried to help Christian pilgrims that caused most of the trouble. Instead of sending ambassadors to negotiate some kind of peaceful agreement, he called on the Christian nobles of Europe and their armies to go to war with the Muslims from the Holy Land and bring that region under Christian control. Urban proclaimed,

> *God [urges] you as heralds of Christ to repeatedly urge men of all ranks whatsoever, knights as well as foot-soldiers, rich and poor, to hasten to exterminate this vile race from our lands and to aid the Christian inhabitants in time ... Christ commands it. For all those going [there] will be [forgiven] of sins if they come to the end of [their lives] while either marching by land or crossing the sea, or in fighting [Muslims].*[14]

Urban's call, which included the Latin words for "God wills it," launched the First Crusade, which lasted from 1095 to 1099. Tens of thousands of people from all across Europe followed various leaders in huge marches that moved eastward across Europe. Some gave their allegiance to a priest named Peter the Hermit, who claimed that Jesus himself had come to him and encouraged the war. Other priests led their own groups of crusaders, as did a number of dukes and other nobles recruited by the pope. Altogether, as few as 30,000 and as many as 70,000 men had traveled to the Middle East by 1097 and were accompanied by thousands of squires, merchants, and laborers.

It is hard to believe that so many people left their families and jobs behind to fight—and possibly die—in a strange, faraway place. However, the Roman Catholic Church held extraordinary power over the hearts and minds of Europeans in the medieval era. The vast majority of the crusading knights and foot soldiers, as well as the civilians who followed them, were filled with genuine religious devotion. They believed that their faith was the only true faith and must be defended to the

Pope Urban II urged Christians to go to war with Muslims.

death. In their view, God had called on them to go to the Holy Land to fight, and afterward to pray, on the very ground where Jesus and his disciples had once walked.

Western Barbarians

Motivated by such religious enthusiasm, the crusaders captured Jerusalem in 1099. One of the attackers, a Frenchman named Fulcher of Chartres, later penned a description of the event, which read in part:

> *The [Christian] leaders ordered scaling ladders to be made, hoping that by a brave assault it might be possible to surmount [climb] the walls by means of the ladders and thus take the city, God helping ... A splendid assault was made on the city from all sides ... but it was discovered that the city could not be entered by the use of ladders ... it was ordered that siege machines be constructed by the artisans, so that by moving them close to the wall we might accomplish our purpose.*[15]

The siege was eventually successful, and after massacring thousands of people in Jerusalem, the Europeans took charge of the city and set up several small Christian states in the area. Collectively, these principalities were called the Outremer, or "lands overseas." However, the Christians could not hold on to Jerusalem. It was recaptured by Muslims in 1187, and it became clear that the Outremer was in danger as well. Europeans responded by launching more Crusades with the goal of retaking Jerusalem and protecting the crusader states in the area. Modern scholars still debate the total number of expeditions that can be identified as full-scale Crusades, but most agree that there were as many as nine. Ultimately, however, these expeditions failed to maintain a permanent European position. By the late 1200s, all the states in the Outremer had fallen. Hundreds of years of fighting, and countless deaths, had amounted to nothing.

The thousands of soldiers from the opposing Muslim armies who were killed and the inhabitants of Jerusalem who were massacred were not the only casualties of these holy wars. It became common practice, for instance, for crusaders on the march to slaughter Jews living in European cities situated on the way to the Holy Land. Thousands of Jewish people—men, women,

"A RACE UTTERLY ALIENATED FROM GOD"

As part of his effort to convince European Christians to launch a holy war to gain control of the Holy Land, Pope Urban II cited numerous atrocities supposedly committed by Muslims against Christians. It is likely that most of these incidents were either false or exaggerated. The pope stated in part:

> *From the confines of Jerusalem and the city of Constantinople a horrible tale has gone forth … namely, that a race from the kingdom of the Persians … a race utterly alienated [removed] from God … has invaded the lands of those Christians and has depopulated them by the sword, pillage and fire; it has led away a part of the captives into its own country, and a part it has destroyed by cruel tortures; it has either entirely destroyed the churches of God or [taken them over] for the rites of their own religion. They destroy the altars, after having defiled them with their uncleanness … Let the holy sepulchre [tomb] of the Lord our Saviour, which is possessed by unclean nations, especially incite you, and the holy places which are now … irreverently polluted with their filthiness.*[1]

1. Pope Urban II at the Council of Clermont, delivered November 27, 1095, in *The First Crusade: The Chronicle of Fulcher of Chartres and Other Source Materials*, Edward Peters, ed. Philadelphia, PA: University of Pennsylvania Press, 1998, p. 27.

and children—suffered torture and met hideous deaths. Any Christians who tried to save them were killed alongside them.

Many European historians, poets, and authors attempted to portray these wars and massacres as positive. Poems, novels, and eventually films all tended to depict the Crusades not only as necessary but also as exciting adventures. This distorted vision obscures the more terrible truth. "Through the haze of legend," one historian wrote, "the Crusades are remembered as a romantic quest by noble knights wearing crimson crosses. In reality, the Crusades were a sickening nightmare of slaughter, rape, looting, and chaos … The crusaders killed nearly as many Christians and Jews as they did Muslims."[16]

Large numbers of Muslims did die in the Crusades. The survivors passed on their own, quite negative version of these wars to later generations. The common view in Islamic cities

The city of Jerusalem has been the location for a lot of religiously motivated bloodshed.

and states in following centuries was that the pure and holy Muslim society was assaulted by Christian barbarians. This attitude has periodically fueled anti-Western feeling among some Muslims, and it continues to do so. Shortly before ordering the invasion of Iraq in 2003, for example, U.S. president George W. Bush remarked to the press about his ongoing crusade against terrorists. His intended meaning was a righteous campaign to capture and punish a band of criminals, but Muslims around the world immediately interpreted the remark as an insensitive reference to a holy war against any and all who practice Islam.

Catholics versus Protestants: The Thirty Years' War

The devastating consequences of the Crusades included numerous instances of vandalism, looting, and murder that took place in European cities as the crusader armies marched eastward. Many of these same cities suffered again from religiously motivated violence only a few centuries later. From 1618 to 1648, large portions of Europe were destroyed by one of the most destructive wars fought in the world up to that time. Later called the Thirty Years' War, the conflict was sparked by religious differences between Catholics and Protestants in Germany. At the time, Germany was not a united country, as it is today, but was made up of several small, independent rival states that were established as either part of the Catholic League or Protestant Union. When some Protestant noblemen tossed two Catholic priests out of a palace window in the city of Prague, an army raised by the Catholic League slaughtered a group of Protestants.

As the war commenced in 1618, the strongest of the German Catholic princes, Ferdinand II, made the situation worse by launching a large-scale religious persecution. It was designed to eliminate every Protestant from the German region and secure for the Catholics all the land and political power. Local Protestants quickly responded by appealing for aid from the rulers of other European nations, and Denmark, Sweden, France, Spain, and other countries got involved. While the conflict began with religious intolerance, it slowly became more centered on the rivalry between France and the House of Hapsburg, the most powerful house of the Holy Roman Empire, for political power.

At first, the many armies attacked only enemy forces, but as time went on, many of the soldiers set off to do their own individual violence and raided both Catholic and Protestant villages at will, spreading destruction and misery far and wide. The destruction of the Protestant German town of Magdeburg is recalled in this eyewitness account:

> *Then was there naught but beating and burning, plundering, torture, and murder. Most especially was every one of the enemy bent on securing much [treasure] ... the great and splendid city that had stood like a fair princess in the land was now ... given over to the flames, and thousands of innocent men, women, and children, in the midst of a horrible din of heartrending shrieks and cries, were tortured and put to death in so cruel and shameful a manner that no words would suffice to describe [it].*[17]

It has been estimated that more than 20,000 residents of Magdeburg were massacred, leaving just a few hundred terrorized survivors behind in the city's charred ruins. Additionally, the war caused the destruction of large tracts of farmland, orchards, and vineyards, resulting in areas of famine and starvation. Debilitating diseases, including typhus, dysentery, and bubonic plague, spread through Germany, Italy, and other areas, wiping out thousands more ordinary citizens.

The Thirty Years' War finally ended in 1648 with the signing of the Treaty of Westphalia. This war, caused by religious hatred and the desire for power, ended up having momentous consequences for later generations of Europeans and Americans. First, Germany emerged from the war in a state of utter devastation and as disunited as ever. Local bitterness over the destruction caused by outsiders later

Ferdinand II attempted to kill all Protestants who prevented Catholics from gaining German political power.

contributed to the growth of militant German nationalism, an important factor in World Wars I and II. Meanwhile, Spain, once one of Europe's strongest nations, lost much power and influence, while France emerged as the continent's dominant power.

Another far-reaching consequence of the war was the way it affected the development of political ideas in the century that followed. When the Founding Fathers of the new United States drew up the Constitution in the late 1700s, the horrors of the Thirty Years' War were still fresh in their minds. They instituted strict separation of church and state, partly as a way of avoiding such destructive wars based on religious differences.

Israeli-Palestinian Conflict

Although the United States made sure to separate issues of religion and government in order to avoid bloodshed, other, older parts of the world have not been as fortunate. One of the most bitter ongoing disputes of this kind is between Arabs and Israelis. From 1948, when the modern nation of Israel was established, to the present day, several violent wars have been fought between Arabs and Jews; Palestinian Arab suicide bombers have frequently attacked Israeli towns, and the Israeli military has struck out at Palestinians. Both sides claim a historical connection to Israel and the rights to settle on the land. Both sides claim that God supports their presence on the land, and both sides have lost thousands of lives, both military and civilian.

As of the 21st century, both the Israeli government and the Palestine Liberation Organization have made attempts to establish peace. In 2007, there was support for a two-state solution, which means the creation of a separate Palestinian state right next to the State of Israel. The amount of violence that has occurred over the whole duration of the conflict, however, has made it difficult for both sides to trust each other. Peace negotiations have been mediated by an international group of countries known as the Quartet on the Middle East; the Quartet consists of the United States, Russia, the European Union, and the United Nations. As of 2018, many different plans for peace in this part of the world have been proposed.

Muslims versus Christians in Sudan

Religiously motivated violence waged over geographic disagreement has also claimed the lives of thousands in Sudan, one of Africa's largest countries. The civil wars that troubled Sudan in the 20th century grew out of religious, ethnic, and political problems that began in the 19th century. Egypt took control of the northern part of Sudan in 1820, but when the Egyptians attempted to extend their control farther south in the 1870s, they encountered resistance. Egyptians called on British military general Charles George Gordon to help organize the region.

Gordon served as a Christian governor of Sudan for the Egyptians. In 1885, Gordon was killed when a Muslim extremist named Muhammad Ahmad, known as the Mahdi, or "enlightened one," led a rebellion and captured the

General Charles George Gordon is shown here.

AGENTS OF GOD

One of the major incidents that fueled hatred between Muslims and Christians was the faceoff between two larger-than-life figures at the battle in Khartoum, the capital of Sudan, in 1884 and 1885. Britain's General Gordon, as governor of Sudan for the Egyptians in the 1870s, was a fundamentalist Christian who saw himself as an agent of God. His opponent at Khartoum, Muhammad Ahmad, a Sudanese Muslim, was an Islamic fundamentalist who claimed to be the Mahdi, a figure similar to Jesus Christ in Islam. The self-proclaimed Mahdi decided that the Egyptians and British were corrupt and must be driven out of Sudan. He defeated several Egyptian armies that were sent to stop him. In 1884, Gordon was asked to go to Khartoum and organize its evacuation, but he was trapped there when the Mahdi's forces attacked. On January 26, 1885, the city fell after a 10-month-long siege, and Gordon was killed in the fighting.

major Sudanese city of Khartoum. The Egyptians then abandoned Sudan, where the Mahdi set up a fundamentalist Islamic state. That regime was short-lived, however, because the British and Egyptians re-invaded Sudan in the late 1890s, and the country became a British colony. As long as the British ruled Sudan, tensions between the Muslim north and Christian south remained under control. However, in 1955, the British announced that they were planning to grant the region its independence the following year. Fearing oppression by the northern Muslims, some of the southern tribes rebelled, and, as the British withdrew, a major civil war broke out. That bloody conflict raged until a peace agreement was signed in 1972, but not without leaving half a million people dead and more than 750,000 homeless.

The truce between the warring groups did not last long. In 1983, Sudanese president Gaafar Muhammad al-Nimeiry, a Muslim, imposed a series of harsh Islamic laws on the entire country, including the severing of hands as punishment for theft and other minor crimes. Many people around the world, including other Muslims, protested that imposing these laws violated the human rights of the Sudanese Christians in the south, which had been granted a sort of independence by the 1972 agreement. Al-Nimeiry and his followers, however, disagreed. The result was another religiously motivated, prolonged, and deadly civil war. Around 250,000 southern Sudanese died in 1988

Gaafar al-Nimeiry was a Sudanese president who practiced violent, extremist Islam.

alone. By 2005, when a treaty finally established a fragile peace, more than 2 million Sudanese citizens had been killed. That same year, a new rebellion erupted in Darfur, a province in western Sudan. The new conflict saw violent Arab militia groups fighting against local black settlers in Darfur, but it was motivated more by racial and ethnic disputes than by religious differences.

The religious war in Sudan clearly shows that the tensions that brought about the Crusades nearly a thousand years before had not vanished. Christians and Muslims still fight to the death for land and power in various corners of the globe, and they are willing to die over their religious differences.

CHAPTER FOUR

HISTORIC HATRED

Sometimes, the worst acts of violence are not motivated by political power or social reform, but simply committed out of hate. Millions of individuals have been killed solely based on their religion, and the history of this hatred often goes back thousands of years. Christians have historically been both the culprits and the victims of religious hatred. In the year 64, the emperor Nero burned hundreds of Christians to death for supposedly starting a large fire that destroyed parts of Rome. This started an anti-Christian trend that lasted for 300 years. Later, Christians came into power and took their revenge, vandalizing pagan temples. Christians also began killing Jews because they believed Jews were all to blame for the crucifixion of Jesus Christ.

Since the first millennium BC, Jewish people have been hated, persecuted, and killed. The term "anti-Semitism" means hatred for and discrimination against Jews. This feeling has come from a deep-seated ignorance about what Jews historically believe and how they worship. The persecution of Jewish people is a tragic example of how destructive blind religious hatred can be, all across history and into the modern world.

Lethal Religious Prejudice

Some of the worst wars, mass murders, and other outbreaks of violence in history have been motivated by senseless religious extremism that is not rooted in anything but hate. Often, the roots of such hatred are found in an event that occurred hundreds or even thousands of years earlier.

In 64 AD, Christianity was still a new and small religious sect in the Roman Empire. The emperor Nero accused the Christians of igniting a great fire that destroyed large portions of the city of Rome that year. Hundreds of Christians were tied to large crosses or stakes, shot with arrows, or burned to death.

These killings were the first of many anti-Christian persecutions carried out by the Romans in the three centuries that followed. In the late 300s, when Christians finally prevailed and took over Rome's government, they turned the tables. It became common for crowds of Christian Romans to seek revenge on non-Christian Romans by vandalizing pagan temples. Later, in medieval and modern times, Christians killed many Jews because of the false belief that all Jews, no matter when or where they were born, were responsible for the death of Jesus Christ. Part of this hostility toward Jewish people may

The Star of David is a recognizable symbol of Jewish identity.

also have originated from an attempt by early Christians to distance themselves from a people widely viewed as fanatical and rebellious. A succession of foreign peoples, including Babylonians, Greeks, and Romans, occupied the Jewish homeland in what is now Israel in the late first millennium BC and early first millennium AD. The Jews, constantly rebelling and attempting to regain their independence, became known as troublemakers. For some Christians (after they split from Judaism in the mid- to late first century), denouncing the Jews was one way of emphasizing that they themselves were no longer Jewish.

Ever since the ancient Jewish kingdoms of Israel and Judah were destroyed by the Assyrians and Babylonians in the first millennium BC, the Jews have suffered from hatred and discrimination. Anti-Semitism has consistently stemmed from ignorance or misconceptions. Tragically, these misperceptions have led to mindless killing.

Continued Blame

Hatred for Jews among Christians originated long before the Crusades. Although Jesus and his earliest followers were all Jews, medieval Christians—self-proclaimed followers of Jesus—came to despise the Jews. The notion that the Jewish people had aided the Romans in crucifying Jesus Christ in Jerusalem around the year AD 30 was the basis of Christian anti-Semitism. Therefore, when Christians took over the leadership of the Roman state in the fourth and fifth centuries, anti-Semitic acts became commonplace. The authorities, who were nearly all Christians, did nothing to punish the perpetrators. When a Christian bishop incited a mob to burn down a Jewish synagogue, Ambrose, one of the leading Christian bishops of the late fourth century, asked, "Who cares if a synagogue—home of insanity and un-belief—is destroyed?"[18]

Many Christian bishops spread hateful words about followers of Judaism. One of Ambrose's contemporaries, John Chrysostom, who served as bishop of both Antioch and Constantinople, delivered a famous series of anti-Semitic speeches. "The difference between the Jews and us is not a small one, is it?" Chrysostom asked. "They crucified the Christ whom you adore as God. Do you see how great the difference is?" He later continued,

> *[Jews] live for their bellies, they gape for the things of this world, their condition is no better than that of pigs or goats because of their wanton ways and excessive gluttony. They know*

ANGRY WORDS

Among the many texts that encouraged violence against Jews in the Middle Ages were the widely quoted anti-Semitic lectures of the fourth-century Christian bishop John Chrysostom, excerpted below:

> *Do you see that demons dwell in their souls and that these demons are more dangerous than the ones of old? And this is very reasonable … Do you not shudder to come into the same place with men possessed, who have so many unclean spirits, who have been [raised] amid slaughter and bloodshed? Must you share a greeting with them and exchange a bare word? Must you not turn away from them since they are the common disgrace and infection of the whole world? Have they not come to every form of wickedness? … They sacrificed their own sons and daughters to demons … What else do you wish me to tell you? Shall I tell you of their plundering, their [jealousy], their abandonment of the poor, their thefts, their cheating in trade?*[1]

1. Quoted in Shlomo Simonsohn, *The Jews of Italy: Antiquity*. Leiden, The Netherlands: Brill, 2014, p. 287.

> *but one thing: to fill their bellies and be drunk … The synagogue is less deserving of honor than any inn. It is not merely a lodging place for robbers and cheats but also for demons. This is true not only of the synagogues but also of the souls of the Jews.*[19]

The anti-Semitic rants of Chrysostom and other Christian leaders not only instigated violence against Jews then, but after Rome's fall in the fifth and sixth centuries, medieval Christians preserved these hateful writings and used them as excuses to continue violence against Jews. Some Christians also circulated horrifying—and false—stories about Jews. One common tale was that Jewish people kidnapped Christian children and killed them in bloody secret rituals. Though these stories were made up, many Christians had been raised to readily believe them. As a result, whenever a Christian child was found dead of unknown causes, suspicions immediately fell on local Jews. In city after city across Europe, for centuries, Jews were routinely slaughtered by the dozens, hundreds, and sometimes thousands to atone for murders they had not committed. Jews were killed even when there was no hard

CRIMES UNCOMMITTED

Across medieval Europe, charges of infanticide—the killing of babies—against Jews was widespread. In 1255, in Lincoln, England, the body of an eight-year-old Christian boy was found in the well of a Jewish family. Rumors immediately spread that local Jews had kidnapped the boy, fattened him with milk and bread, and then invited Jews from far and wide to witness his brutal execution by crucifixion. Though these charges were untrue, 18 Jews were tortured and hanged. In 1294, in Bern, Switzerland, some Christians claimed that a local Jewish person had collected several Christian babies in a sack and was eating them one by one. As a result of this, all the Jews in Bern were either killed or driven away with only the clothes on their backs. In Trent, Italy, in 1475, almost every Jew in the city was tortured or burned alive after a hysterical charge that they had kidnapped and sacrificed a Christian infant named Simon.

evidence of a crime. In Blois, France, in 1171, for example, a Christian claimed he saw some Jewish people throw a child's body into a river. No body was ever found and no children had been reported missing, yet dozens of local Jewish leaders were rounded up, locked in a wooden shed, and burned alive.

False Accusations

Throughout the Middle Ages, increasingly outrageous accusations were made against the Jews by Christians. A common charge involved the "host," or the wafer that represented the body of Jesus Christ in the Christian sacrament of Holy Communion. Rumors circulated that Jews sometimes stole the sacred wafers and drove nails through them to symbolically crucify Jesus once again and that the wafers bled or cried out in pain at the moment they were pierced. Incited to violence by these accusations, Christian mobs periodically attacked the Jewish quarters of many European cities. In 1298, after a Christian priest in Nuremberg, Germany, claimed that Jews had stolen the host, an angry crowd rushed into the city's Jewish quarter and massacred hundreds of people. That same year, a German knight who believed similar stories led a regiment of soldiers in raids on more than 140 Jewish communities; thousand of Jews, including women and children, were killed without mercy. There was also a massacre in Brussels, Belgium, in 1370. After someone claimed that a Jew had broken a host wafer in half, enraged

Many Jewish people were accused of disrespecting Jesus Christ in the Middle Ages. Countless drawings show that these people were then burned alive all across Europe.

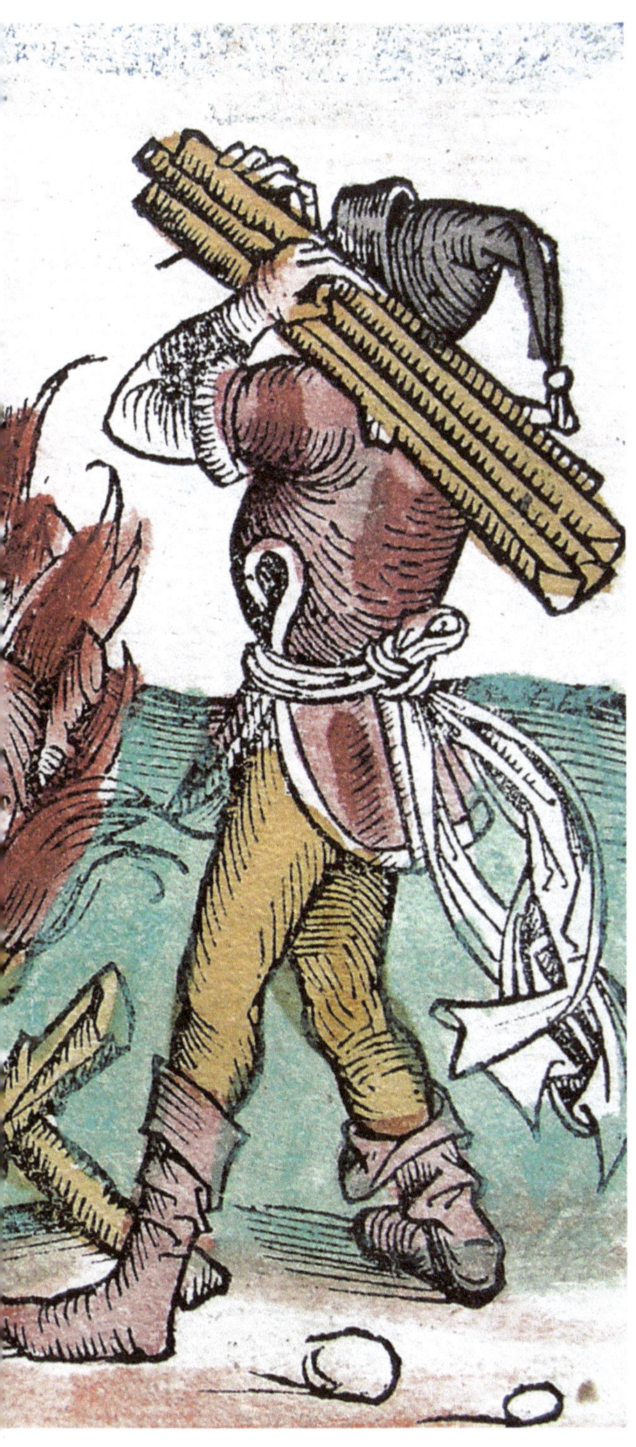

mobs of Christians annihilated the city's entire Jewish community by either killing its members or driving them from the city.

Still another false accusation against Jews in the medieval centuries was that they poisoned Christian wells and other water supplies in an effort to achieve revenge on Christians and wipe out Christian communities. One of the earliest reports of this crime occurred in France in 1320. An outbreak of an unknown disease struck, and then a rumor spread that local Jews, Muslims, and lepers had conspired to poison water supplies, causing the sickness. None of these claims were accurate.

The Black Death

The charges of well poisoning against Jews became much more widespread and hysterical only a few years later. In 1347 and 1348, the bubonic plague, which many called the Black Death, struck Europe with catastrophic effects. Millions were infected and died horrible deaths in a frighteningly short period. Desperate to find some explanation or assign blame for the catastrophe, many people believed untrue rumors that Jews had poisoned wells across the continent. Any Jewish person could be accused of poisoning a town, and the largely Christian residents would rush to execute them, even before they were put to trial. This resulted in countless deaths, despite the fact that Jews were suffering from the plague equally. According to one account

All across Europe, Jews were unjustly murdered after being accused of causing the Black Death.

from a German cleric of the time,

> *The persecution of the Jews began in November 1348, and the first outbreak in Germany was at Sölden, where all the Jews were burnt on the strength of a rumor that they had poisoned wells and rivers … When these were [tortured] they confessed that they had themselves sprinkled poison or poisoned rivers … All the Jews between Cologne and Austria were burnt and killed for this crime, young men and maidens and the old along with the rest. And blessed be God who [stopped] the ungodly who were plotting the extinction of his church … In Zofingen they were seized and some [tortured], then in Stuttgart they were all burnt … In Horw they were burnt in a pit.*[20]

In 1349, in Frankfurt, Germany, an army of Christians assaulted the local Jewish neighborhood and massacred hundreds of people. In some other

European cities, local dukes and other Christian nobles sent their soldiers to help slaughter Jews. In all, European Christians perpetrated at least 350 mass murders of Jews in the span of only three or four years during the great plague. Most of these crimes were documented by Christian writers, sometimes in excruciating detail and often with moral justification.

The Holocaust

Anti-Semitism and religiously motivated attacks on Jews continued in Europe and elsewhere well into the 20th century. The most well known and worst crime against Jewish people occurred during World War II. This event was the Holocaust, the attempt by Adolf Hitler and his Nazi Party to wipe out Judaism through systematic genocide. Although Hitler's personal motivation for this mass murder was mainly racial or ethnic, it was enabled by religious hatred. The Holocaust was built on top of centuries of religious persecution of Jews by Christians. One scholar explained,

Millions of Jews were killed in gas chambers at death camps such as Auschwitz.

For century after century after century, the Christian church had designated the people to be despised: the religious believers called Jews, the "Christ-killers," the "enemies of God" ... When popes ordered Jews to wear [identification] badges and live in ghettos ... it told the populace that these [outcasts] were unfit to live among decent folk ... Thus, when Adolf Hitler needed a scapegoat group to rally the discontented majority to his cause and catapult himself to power, natural victims clearly marked

by the church were at his disposal. The Christian public, not only in Germany but also throughout Europe, was predisposed to receive the Nazi message of Jew-hatred.[21]

Another historian agreed, pointing out Hitler's historical precedents:

Everything Hitler did to the Jews, all the horrible, unspeakable misdeeds, had already been done to the smitten people before by the Christian churches, especially the Catholic Church.

The isolation of the Jews in ghetto camps, the wearing of the yellow [identification badge], the burning of Jewish books, and finally the burning of the people—Hitler learned it all from the Catholic Church. However, the Church burned the Jewish women and children alive, while Hitler granted them a quicker death, choking them first with gas.[22]

Millions of Jewish people were forced into gas chambers and killed during the Holocaust; many thousands were shot, starved, or killed by other means. To achieve this, Hitler's secret police captured Jews from across Europe and forced them onto overcrowded trains, shipping them to concentration camps. These camps were facilities designed for extermination, and many were located in Nazi-occupied Poland. These death camps were equipped with gas chambers. The chambers at the Treblinka camp killed up to 200 victims at a time; the camp at Auschwitz eventually boasted a gas chamber that could accommodate ten times that number. At its peak, Auschwitz murdered thousands of people every day. In all, nearly 6 million European Jews went to their deaths before the camps were

The neighboring countries of India and Pakistan have a short, difficult, and violent history.

dismantled and Allied forces defeated the Nazis in World War II.

India versus Pakistan

Although the Jewish people have long been a target of religiously motivated massacres and hate crimes in Europe and other Western countries, the East has also experienced its share of hatred. In early modern times, mutual distrust and hatred among Indian Hindus, Muslims, and Sikhs periodically erupted in violence. When the British took control of the Indian subcontinent in the 1800s, authorities managed to keep the peace most of the time among members of these opposing religious groups, but in 1947, bowing to pressure from both inside and outside India, the British granted the colony its independence. Many Indians were glad to see the British leave. However, the Hindus and Muslims who were attempting to form a coalition government could not reach a mutual agreement, and religious tensions rose across the country. Fearing the outbreak of civil war, the British agreed to divide the former colony into two new nations: India, which would be ruled by Hindus, and Pakistan, which would be controlled by Muslims.

Though the division was an effort to establish peace, it unleashed a storm of unrest, chaos, and violent conflict. Most Hindus living in the newly created Pakistan abandoned their homes and moved to India. Meanwhile, many Muslims living in India joined a giant mass migration into Pakistan. Much of the Punjab, the ancestral homeland of the Sikhs, was now part of Pakistan, forcing many Sikhs in that area to leave and make new homes in the new India. In an atmosphere of dislocation, in which everyone resented everyone else, attacks and killings were inevitable. Rioting, burning, looting, beatings, property seizures, and outright murder became commonplace. Brutal massacres wiped out entire families and even whole villages. Between 500,000 and 1 million people died in the violence that accompanied the creation of India and Pakistan.

Teaching to Hate

Eventually, the initial violence of the division of countries subsided, but India and Pakistan still struggled to trust each other. The hatred between Hindus, Muslims, and Sikhs in the region remained, threatening violence for the smallest reasons. In 1989, in northern India, a dispute over whether a certain piece of land should house a Hindu temple or a Muslim mosque touched off a riot that killed hundreds.

One reason why religious violence occurs decade after decade is that people on each side teach hatred to new generations of children. Both Indian and Pakistani schoolbooks, for example, have twisted or even fabricated historical facts, often placing the blame for unrest on members of rival faiths. One pro-Muslim Pakistani text reads,

> *The religion of the Hindus did not teach them good things, Hindus did not respect women … The Hindu has always been an enemy of Islam … The foundation of the Hindu setup was based on injustice and cruelty … Hindus always desired to crush the Muslims as a nation. Several attempts were made by the Hindus to erase Muslim culture and civilisation … Islam gives a message of peace and brotherhood … There is no such concept in Hinduism.*[23]

When children are taught to hate other religions from an early age, it is difficult to not then have a country

GANDHI

Amid all the horrific violence and bloodshed between Hindus and Muslims in India in the 1940s, one man stood out and became a symbol of peace and tolerance. He was the world renowned pacifist and humanitarian Mohandas Gandhi. Widely respected by nearly all Indians, no matter their religion or background, he frequently helped negotiate truces among opposing groups by going on hunger strikes. His nonviolent protests help Indians achieve independence from Britain, a long-held dream for the oppressed nation. Respect for Gandhi bordered on reverence. The countless people he inspired gave him the title Mahatma, which can be translated as "great soul."

Gandhi was greatly respected by many and is honored globally for his efforts toward peace.

full of intolerant adults. Not all Hindus and Muslims have fallen for these attempts to maintain hatred and intolerance, however. Dozens of moderate, tolerant voices have arisen in the wake of violence and religious oppression, each speaking to end the culture of distrust and hatred that has plagued the two nations. Many have argued that if the educational systems of both countries improved—and taught a respectful view of history and other religions—then the mutual hatred would die out.

EPILOGUE

INTERFAITH VIOLENCE

Religiously motivated violence is not limited to hatred between members of opposing denominations. Violence, unfortunately, also has a historic presence within those denominations themselves. Fundamentalists in a given religion often find just as much fault in the members of the same faith who interpret the same scripture differently as they do in members of other faiths. Sometimes, these disagreements result in fatal violence.

Catholics and Protestants, in particular, have a history of bad blood. Although both religions are Christian, there are enough differences between them to cause friction. The biggest difference being that Catholics follow the pope, while Protestants do not. The bitterness between the two religious groups has caused wars that continued into modern times. Perhaps even more infamous is the hostility between two different groups of Muslims, the Shiites and the Sunnis. They disagree on who exactly has the authority handed down from the prophet Muhammad, and this has led to extreme bloodshed that has persisted in the modern world.

Sunni Against Shiite

The violence between the Sunnis and the Shiites in Iraq can be traced in large part to the policies of the former ruler of that nation, Saddam Hussein, and his relations with neighboring Iran. Most of the inhabitants of Iran and Iraq are Muslims. The vast majority of Iranians are Shiites. In Iraq, the population is mixed. About 55 percent of Iraqis are Shiites, while roughly 40 percent of Iraqis are Sunnis, and the remaining 5 percent are non-Muslims. Though the Shiites have always been in the majority in Iraq, they never controlled the government. Both Saddam's predecessors and he

Saddam Hussein was the president of Iraq from 1979 to 2003.

himself made sure that the Sunnis held all political power and occupied every important political post in the country.

Saddam and his Sunni followers did not like the fact that a Shiite-dominated state—Iran—shares a major border with Iraq. The shah (ruler) of Iran, however, was a secular leader who had Western allies, so Iraq refrained from attacking Iran. In 1979, the shah was overthrown by Shiites who instituted a strict theocracy (which is a government ruled by religious leaders and religious law). Soon afterward, Iraq attacked Iran, and a bloody, decade-long conflict ensued between Iranian Shiites and Iraqi Sunnis (aided by Iraqi Shiites, who felt more allegiance to Iraqi Sunnis than to Iranian Shiites). More than a million people died in the brutal, chaotic fighting. Hoping the Iranian Shiite theocracy would be toppled, U.S. leaders sided with Saddam and supplied him with weapons.

Later, however, the Americans began to oppose Saddam. In 1991, Saddam invaded the small nation of Kuwait and claimed it as part of Iraq. An international coalition led by the United States drove Saddam's forces out of Kuwait, but the dictator's regime survived. In 2003, President George W. Bush, assisted by British leaders, ordered an invasion of Iraq intended to remove Saddam from power and establish a democracy in that country. The initial attack succeeded, and Saddam Hussein and his top followers were stripped of power. Many Shiites rejoiced. The problem was that the Sunnis were not happy to give up their power. Aided by terrorists from other Muslim countries, some of the Sunnis launched a revolt aimed at driving the Americans out and reinstating Sunni control of the country. Despite the best efforts of America and its allies, there is an ongoing violent conflict in Iraq between Sunnis and Shiites, which has led to many deaths.

War on Mecca

The recent fighting between Shiites and Sunnis in Iraq is certainly not the first example of Muslims fighting Muslims. One of the worst examples of this violence in recent times occurred in Saudi Arabia in 1979. Ever since Muhammad established Islam in the seventh century, the Saudis have been the caretakers of the religion's holiest shrines, located in Mecca and Medina. Every year, millions of Muslims travel to Mecca to complete a sacred pilgrimage called the *hajj*. Among other rituals, they walk seven times around the Kaaba, a sacred cube-shaped monument said to date back to the time of the prophet Abraham.

Because Saudi Arabia is home to these and other shrines sacred to Muslims everywhere, Saudi authorities feel obligated to protect the

In the middle of this photograph is the Kaaba—the holiest shrine in Islam.

shrines at all costs, even against fellow Muslims. In 1979, a Sunni named Juhayman al-Utaybi rose up and threatened the integrity of the holy places. Al-Utaybi thought that Muslims should reject all non-Muslim entertainment and that women did not need to be educated. He advocated for very strict social laws. Hoping to force these and other changes on both Sunnis and Shiites in Saudi Arabia, al-Utaybi and 200 of his loyal followers armed themselves with guns and took over Mecca's Grand Mosque. The tens of thousands of pilgrims then visiting the shrines were told that they must join al-Utaybi's movement or leave the holy site and never return. Al-Utaybi believed he was Islam's new messiah and that Muslims everywhere would flock to his cause. However, five days after he seized the mosque, the Saudi government sent in military commandos. After nine days of fighting, more than 200 people were killed and al-Utaybi and his leading followers were captured and beheaded.

In addition to the crisis in Mecca, Saudi authorities were forced to deal with an even more destructive confrontation later in 1979. For some time, the government had banned a traditional Shiite religious ritual: the festival of Ashura, which celebrates the martyrdom of Muhammad's grandson Hussein. However, Shiites in 1979 decided that they would defy this ban. Their celebration provoked a response by Saudi police, who moved in to make arrests. In turn, the actions of the police set off deadly riots, during which many stores and cars were destroyed and more than a dozen Shiites were killed.

Fringe Division

Although Shiite Muslims have been persecuted and politically dominated in Saudi Arabia, Iraq, and other countries, the Shiites have also fought among themselves from time to time. The Shiites have opposed followers' attempts to break with tradition, introduce new religious ideas, or form new branches of Shiite Islam. The most famous and tragic example of violence sparked by Shiites challenging the basic tenets of Islam is that of the persecution of the Baha'i in the 19th and 20th centuries. The Baha'i began as a fringe branch of Islam and remained a part of that faith for many years. Only later did they come to see their religion as separate from Islam. Today, the Baha'i faith is one of the world's fastest-growing religions, with millions of global followers. Members believe in the existence of a single, all-powerful god and that all people, including women, are equal in God's sight. They also revere the prophets of all the major religions—including Moses, Abraham, Buddha, Muhammad, and Jesus—as various manifestations of God.

For people who routinely preach brotherhood, tolerance, and universal

The Baha'i use a symbol of a nine-pointed star because the number nine is associated with perfection and unity.

BAHA'I PERSECUTION MADE LEGAL

Modern persecutions of the Baha'i in Iran have been allowed by Iranian legal authorities. In 1983, a leading Iranian Shiite judge named Hujjat u'l-Islam Qaza'i stated,

> *The Iranian Nation has risen in accordance with Koranic teachings and by the will of God has determined to establish the government of God on earth. Therefore, it cannot tolerate the perverted [Baha'i] who are the instruments of Satan and followers of the Devil … It is absolutely certain in the Islamic Republic of Iran there is no place whatsoever for [Baha'i]. Before it is too late the [Baha'i believers] should recant [their religion]. Otherwise, the day will come when the Islamic Nation will deal with the [Baha'i] in accordance with its religious obligations and will.*[1]

1. Quoted in Per-Olof Åkerdahl, *Bahā'ī Identity and the Concept of Martyrdom*. Uppsala, Sweden: Bahá'í-förlaget AB, 2002, p. 101.

peace, the Baha'i have suffered a lot of hate, persecution, and violence, especially in the faith's early years. The religion first appeared in 1844, when an Iranian Shiite holy man proclaimed that he was the Bāb, or "gateway," meaning he was a portal connecting the ordinary world to the divine world. The Bāb claimed that a highly revered ancient preacher, the "Twelfth Imam," spoke to humanity through him. When the Bāb managed to attract an increasingly large following of Shiite Muslims, the conservative Islamic government of Iran became worried. The authorities eventually arrested the Bāb and executed him in 1850.

However, the new branch of Islam the Bāb had initiated did not die with him. In retaliation for this execution, two of the Bāb's followers tried to assassinate the shah of Iran. This act triggered a war that left thousands of Baha'i believers dead, but the surviving members of the movement persevered. A few years later, a man calling himself the Baha'u'llah ("Glory of God") claimed he was a divine messenger. He revitalized the movement. Meanwhile, the Baha'i, who by this time no longer viewed themselves as Muslims, spread their faith to Turkey, Cyprus, and other lands.

Back in Iran, the government never gave up persecuting the Baha'i believers. Many members of the faith were massacred during the 20th century. Perhaps the worst persecution of the Baha'i occurred in Iran in 1955. During Ramadan of that year, a conservative Muslim preacher delivered an angry sermon over the radio, calling on all devout Muslims to root out, attack, and destroy the Baha'i, whom he claimed had disrespected and destroyed Islamic teachings. Responding to these hateful words, mobs of soldiers and civilians destroyed the Baha'i temples and cemeteries across Iran. The Baha'i were beaten and murdered throughout Iran. The violence did not stop until the government of Iran, which had initially supported the oppression of Baha'i believers, stepped in to avoid international criticism.

Huguenot Slaughter

Fighting and killing among members of the same faith has been a recurring feature of Christianity as well as Islam for many centuries. Although the Thirty Years' War, fought between 1618 and 1648, produced the largest single death toll in a Catholic versus Protestant conflict, it was neither the first nor the cruelest example of attempts by Catholics and Protestants to wipe each other out.

About three generations before the outbreak of the Thirty Years' War, some Catholic countries instituted programs designed to rid themselves of Protestants. France and Spain, both predominantly Catholic, signed a treaty in 1559, agreeing to cooperate in harassing and deporting Protestants. What Catholic leaders did not anticipate, however, was the degree to which many Protestants would resist exile. In France alone, eight separate religious wars took place between 1562 and 1598. They are called the Huguenot Wars, after the French word for Calvinist Protestants. Although Catholics committed many atrocities against Huguenots in these conflicts, the Huguenots were frequently equally ruthless and vicious. As one Frenchman wrote in a surviving eyewitness account,

> *It would be impossible to tell you what barbarous cruelties are committed by both sides. Where the Huguenot is master, he ruins the images [of God] and demolishes the [holy] tombs. On the other hand, the Catholic kills, murders and drowns all those whom he knows to be of that sect, until the rivers overflow with them.*[24]

Perhaps the most infamous incident of the French Christian wars was the Massacre of St. Bartholomew's Day in 1572. A French Catholic noblewoman, Catherine de Medici, announced that she wanted to make peace with the Huguenots, so she promised her daughter's hand in marriage to a prominent Huguenot leader, Henry of Navarre. Catherine

The Massacre of St. Bartholomew's Day saw the murder of many Huguenots by the Catholics.

promised safe passage for thousands of Huguenots to travel to Paris for the wedding. However, she also secretly plotted with several Catholic dukes to assassinate a major Huguenot admiral who was scheduled to attend the festivities. This assassination attempt did not succeed. Fearing retaliation by the Huguenots, Catherine and the dukes decided to strike again. On August 24, 1572, a holiday honoring St. Bartholomew, Catholic troops swarmed through Paris's Huguenot neighborhoods, slaughtering men, women, and children. Eyewitness accounts of the massacre have survived, and they describe a brutal scene of lawless and senseless slaughter. Anyone even suspected of Huguenot beliefs was

THE MARCHING SEASON

One Irish Protestant tradition that has consistently irritated Catholics is the marching season. It consists of a series of more than 3,000 parades staged by Protestants between Easter Monday and the end of September. One of the biggest and most controversial marches, held on July 12, commemorates the victory of the Protestant English king William of Orange over the Catholics at the Battle of the Boyne in 1690, an event that solidified Protestant power in Ireland. The Protestant marchers say that they are merely celebrating their cultural heritage, but most Irish Catholics view the marches as arrogant, designed to claim Protestant superiority over the Catholic minority. As a result, in almost every year during the 1980s and 1990s, the marching season resulted in riots, vandalism, and other mayhem in Northern Ireland.

murdered without a second thought, and those responsible were never punished for their actions.

Similar massacres occurred in other French cities. In all, it has been estimated that tens of thousands of Huguenots were killed in the span of a few days—3,000 in Paris alone. Their only "crime" was that they had refused to recognize the pope as their spiritual leader while worshipping Jesus Christ.

Eradicating the Anabaptists

The repeated attempts by Catholics to eradicate the Huguenots and other Protestants in the 1500s and 1600s were certainly violent and cruel, but some historians and religious scholars contend that no single Christian group suffered more at the hands of fellow Christians than the Anabaptists. What made the Anabaptists different from the others was that they were persecuted by both Catholic fundamentalists and other Protestant groups.

The reason many Christian groups opposed the Anabaptists was a religious difference from other denominations. However, in the 1500s, that difference was widely viewed as a disgusting form of blasphemy against God. Unlike most denominations of Christianity, Anabaptists do not believe in baptizing infants. Rather, followers of this sect believe that it is only appropriate to be baptized as an adult. Additionally, many medieval Anabaptists refused to follow certain regulations and government rules, which made them seem like dangerous rebels.

To rid themselves of these allegedly dangerous radicals, other Christians routinely resorted to aggression and violence. In Switzerland, Anabaptists were rounded up and held underwater until they drowned; to their captors, this punishment seemed appropriate, as it symbolized their rejection of classical baptism practices. In Germany, both Catholics and Protestants attacked local Anabaptists. Even Martin Luther, the founder of the Protestant Reformation and himself a religious rebel, joined in condemning Anabaptists to horrible deaths. Some were drowned, others were burned alive, and still others, including children, were beheaded.

In 1534, a group of fleeing Anabaptists seized the German city of Munster. They demanded that all Catholics and Protestants in the city either join them or leave; accordingly, all of the non-Anabaptists departed as quickly as they could. Soon, the former bishop of Munster arrived with an army and besieged the city. After many months of bloody fighting, the Anabaptists of Munster fell, and the victorious Catholic soldiers went on a rampage. Anabaptists in the city were tortured and killed, and other strongholds of the Protestant faith were attacked across Europe. Even after years of persecution, however, some Anabaptists survived. Today, they make up a number of small Protestant sects, including the Mennonites, Amish, and Hutterites.

A Northern Nightmare

Even while they were persecuting Anabaptists, Catholic and Protestant forces in Europe continued to battle each other. One of the worst and most widely publicized troubled areas was Northern Ireland. The animosity there between the two main branches of Christianity began in the 1500s, when Britain's King Henry VIII broke away from the Roman Catholic Church and formed the Protestant Church of England. Henry also forced his new brand of Christianity on Ireland, where at the time the vast majority of people were Catholic. The Irish Catholics resisted, and many were killed. Moreover, similar violent assaults on Irish Catholics continued under Henry's Protestant daughter Elizabeth I, her Protestant successor, James I, and the Puritan dictator Oliver Cromwell.

A major turning point in Ireland's history came when James I settled tens of thousands of Protestants in Ulster, Northern Ireland. For generations to come, many Catholics either hid in caves and makeshift villages in the hills or suffered discrimination as low-level workers on Protestant estates. The division of Catholics and Protestants in Ireland became even more pronounced in 1920, when the British Parliament passed the Government of Ireland Act, which divided Ireland into two separate political units: the predominantly Catholic south and the predominantly

Northern Ireland belongs to the United Kingdom, while southern Ireland is an independent country.

Protestant north. Then, in 1949, the south became a nation separate from Britain—the Republic of Ireland.

In Ulster, still part of Britain, the Catholic minority hoped that the north might eventually join with the south, creating a single Irish state, but most of the Protestants of Ulster did not want such a union. The result was generations of violence between Protestants and Catholics in Ulster. The 1970s witnessed the heaviest bloodshed, but the fighting in the 1980s and 1990s was almost as bad. In 1985, for example, there were dozens of bombings, hundreds of shootings, and nearly 1,000 people wounded. Fortunately—for everyone involved—a truce signed in 1998 is still in force, and people on both sides hope the nightmare of Christians killing and maiming other Christians will not resume.

The Future of Religious Conflict

Religion, despite its positive achievements and potential for good, has inspired hatred, terrorism, mass murder, wars, and other tragedies, and it seems inevitable that it will continue to do so. However, religion also inspires kindness and mercy in billions of people worldwide. Individuals instill religious teachings in their children in order to establish a sense of morality. Religion is the origin and foundation of millions of acts of charity, disaster relief, and refugee aid. Like all human concepts, however, it can be used for evil even if it was not created to do so.

The world has changed greatly since the Crusades, witch hunts, and even the Holocaust. Many strive to achieve a general message of global tolerance, despite any religious differences. The 266th Catholic pope, Francis, teaches Catholicism with an emphasis on mercy and love, not with the aim to overthrow and eradicate rival religions or accuse individuals of heresy. Fewer people are quick to identify themselves as a particular denomination: In the 2010s, a majority of Americans have said they believe in God, but many have rejected religious affiliation. In 1992, 6 percent said they did not identify with a particular religion, while that number had jumped to 22 percent by 2014.

This is not to say that religious conflict will disappear in the foreseeable future. The world is still plagued by plenty of hate, and much of it is focused on the Middle East: Syria has witnessed nearly 500,000 deaths as a result of the occupation of the Islamic State. Life expectancy in Syria has plummeted, and the cost of the ongoing civil war—fueled by Islamic extremism—has cost hundreds of billions of dollars. However, the efforts of many to fight against this terrorism with messages of love are what humanity must focus on going into the future. The Islamic State's goal is to encourage Westerners to hate and fear all Muslims. Many young Muslims who are attracted to ISIS feel excluded and hated.

The best way to combat current and future terrorism and other religiously motivated violence is to show that one is aware of the difference between the majority of believers and the extreme views held by only a few radicals. Acceptance of peaceful members of all religions can go a long way toward preventing future holy wars.

Notes

Introduction: Explaining Religious War

1. Quoted in Bruce Lincoln, *Holy Terrors: Thinking About Religion After September 11*. Chicago, IL: University of Chicago Press, 2003, pp. 96–97.
2. James A. Haught, *Holy Horrors: An Illustrated History of Religious Murder and Madness*. Amherst, NY: Prometheus Books, 2002, pp. xxi–xxii.
3. Steven Weinberg, interview by Margaret Wertheim, *Faith & Reason*, PBS, September 1998. www.pbs.org/faithandreason/transcript/weinframe.html.
4. Quoted in William J. Duiker and Jackson J. Spielvogel, *The Essential World History*. Boston, MA: Cengage Learning, 2016, p. 174.
5. Deuteronomy 20:10–14 (New King James Version).

Chapter One: Religious Fundamentalism

6. Bernard Lewis, *Arabs in History*. Oxford, UK: Oxford University Press, 1993, p. 101.
7. Quoted in Edward S. Ellis and Charles F. Horne, *The Story of the Greatest Nations: From the Dawn of History to the Twentieth Century*. New York, NY: Francis R. Niglutsch, 1901, p. 535.
8. Haught, *Holy Horrors*, p. 76.
9. Quoted in John P. Prendergast, "Cromwell's Conquest and Settlement of Ireland," in *The Dublin Review*, vol. VII, July–October. London, UK: Burns, Lambert & Oates, 1866, p. 442.

Chapter Two: Religious Terror

10. Bernard Lewis, *The Assassins: A Radical Sect in Islam*. New York, NY: Basic Books, 1967, pp. xi–xii.
11. Lewis, *The Assassins*, pp. 139–140.

12. The al Qaeda Manual, Introduction, 2000 (excerpt)" in *The Iraq Papers*, John Ehrenberg, J. Patrick McSherry, et al., eds. Oxford, UK: Oxford University Press, 2010, p. 496.

13. Osama bin Laden, "Jihad Against Jews and Crusaders." Federation of American Scientists. fas.org/irp/world/para/docs/980223-fatwa.htm.

Chapter Three: One Nation, Under God

14. Quoted in George Herring, *An Introduction to the History of Christianity: From the Early Church to the Enlightenment*. London, UK: Continuum, 2006, p. 327.

15. Quoted in James B. Tschen-Emmons, *Artifacts from Medieval Europe*. Santa Barbara, CA: ABC-CLIO, 2015, p. 57.

16. Haught, *Holy Horrors*, p. 19.

17. Quoted in Jackson J. Spielvogel, *Western Civilization: Volume I: To 1715*. Boston, MA: Cengage Learning, 2018, p. 439.

Chapter Four: Historic Hatred

18. Haught, *Holy Horrors*, p. 43.

19. John Chrysostom, *Discourses Against Judaizing Christians*, Paul W. Harkins, trans. Washington, DC: Catholic University of America Press, 2010, pp. 14–15.

20. Quoted in Barbara H. Rosenwein, ed., *Reading the Middle Ages: Sources from Europe, Byzantium, and the Islamic World*. Toronto, Canada: University of Toronto Press, 2014, p. 446.

21. Haught, *Holy Horrors*, pp. 157–158.

22. Dagobert D. Runes, *The War Against the Jew*. Open Road Media, 2015. PDF e-book.

23. Quoted in "'Hindu, Enemy of Islam,'" *Outlook*, October 10, 2005. www.outlookindia.com/magazine/story/hindu-enemy-of-islam/228854.

Epilogue: Interfaith Violence

24. Quoted in John Child, Tim Hodge, Pal Shuter, David Taylor, *Understanding History*, vol. 2. Portsmouth, NH: Heinemann, 1992, p. 32.

For More Information

Books

Byrom, Jamie, and Michael Riley. *The Crusades*. London, UK: Hodder Education, 2013.

This detailed book outlines the causes and effects of the Crusades.

Friedman, Thomas L. *Longitudes and Attitudes: The World in the Age of Terrorism*. New York, NY: Anchor, 2003.

This book is an excellent commentary on the reasons for extremist Muslim hatred of the West and the rise of world terrorism.

Kamen, Henry. *The Spanish Inquisition: A Historical Revision*. New Haven, CT: Yale University Press, 2014.

One of the most famous periods of Catholic religious persecution was the Spanish Inquisition. This book outlines the history, motivations, and long-term effects of the fighting done in the Catholic Church's name.

Mayer, Thomas F. *The Roman Inquisition: A Papal Bureaucracy and Its Laws in the Age of Galileo*. Philadelphia, PA: University of Pennsylvania Press, 2013.

Giving a thorough look at the Roman Inquisition, this book investigates the background of the religious conflict it created.

McCants, William. *The ISIS Apocalypse: The History, Strategy, and Doomsday Vision of the Islamic State*. New York, NY: St. Martin's Press, 2015.

This book offers a detailed history of how ISIS was formed, focusing on the powerful leaders who have made it infamous.

Websites

Islam Guide
www.islam-guide.com
This website is a guide for non-Muslims who want to better understand Islam, which is a way to help prevent future religious clashes.

Jewish Virtual Library
www.jewishvirtuallibrary.org
This website is a digital encyclopedia of Jewish-related topics, including a history of persecutions.

Religious Tolerance
www.religioustolerance.org/var_rel.htm
This website compares and contrasts beliefs in various world religions with a goal of promoting peaceful coexistence.

The September 11 Digital Archive
www.911digitalarchive.org
This website offers a large collection of pictures, audio recordings, news commentaries, and other forms of documentation of the September 11 attacks.

Timeline for the Crusades and Christian Holy War to c.1350
www.usna.edu/Users/history/abels/hh315/crusades_timeline.htm
Hosted by the United States Naval Academy, this website provides context and background for the Crusades.

Index

Picture Credits

Cover DEA PICTURE LIBRARY/Contributor/De Agostini/Getty Images; pp. 6–7 (background) jorisvo/Shutterstock.com; p. 6 (left) ostill/Shutterstock.com; p. 6 (right) Berti123/Shutterstock.com; pp. 7 (top), 70–71 UniversalImagesGroup/Contributor/Universal Images Group/Getty Images; pp. 7 (left), 26–27 Bettmann/Contributor/Bettmann/Getty Images; p. 7 (right) AHMAD AL-RUBAYE/Stringer/AFP/Getty Images; p. 9 Spencer Platt/Staff/Getty Images News/Getty Images; p. 12 Getty Images/Stringer/Getty Images News/Getty Images; pp. 14, 54–55 De Agostini Picture Library/Getty Images; p. 17 Elena Dijour/Shutterstock.com; p. 19 Archive Photos/Stringer/Archive Photos/Getty Images; pp. 22–23 Print Collector/Contributor/Hulton Archive/Getty Images; p. 25 PHAS/Contributor/Universal Images Group/Getty Images; p. 29 GraphicaArtis/Contributor/Archive Photos/Getty Images; p. 30 Fine Art/Contributor/Corbis Historical/Getty Images; p. 34 Transcendental Graphics/Contributor/Archive Photos/Getty Images; p. 37 Print Collector/Contributor/Hulton Fine Art Collection/Getty Images; p. 40 Louise Batalla Duran/Alamy Stock Photo; pp. 42–43 Itai/Wikimedia Commons; pp. 46–47 AP Photo; pp. 48–49 AHMAD AL-RUBAYE/Contributor/AFP/Getty Images; p. 57 Rostislav Glinsky/Shutterstock.com; p. 59 DEA/A. DAGLI ORTI/Contributor/De Agostini Editorial/Getty Images; p. 61 Universal History Archive/Contributor/Universal Images Group/Getty Images; p. 63 Staff/AFP/Getty Images; pp. 66–67 Godong/UIG/Universal Images Group/Getty Images; pp. 72–73 Private Collection/© Look and Learn/Bridgeman Images; pp. 74–75 ullstein bild/Contributor/ullstein bild/Getty Images; p. 76 © iStockphoto.com/hansslegers; p. 78 Dinodia Photos/Contributor/Hulton Archive/Getty Images; p. 81 MIKE NELSON/Staff/AFP/Getty Images; p. 83 AHMAD FAIZAL YAHYA/Shutterstock.com; p. 85 casejustin/Shutterstock.com; pp. 88–89 DEA/G. DAGLI ORTI/Contributor/De Agostini/Getty Images; p. 92 © iStockphoto.com/PeterHermesFurian.

About the Author

Caroline Kennon is a college librarian originally from Yonkers, New York. She received her bachelor's and master's degrees in English from St. Bonaventure University in Western New York and her master's degree in library science from the University at Buffalo. She is an avid reader, a novice cyclist, and a cheese addict. She currently lives in South Buffalo, New York—the winters really aren't that bad.